WALL STREET JOURNAL & USA TODAY BESTSELLING AUTHOR
KB WINTERS

Copyright and Disclaimer

This book is a work of fiction. The names, characters, places and incidents are products of the writer's imagination and have been used fictitiously and are not to be construed as real. Any resemblance to persons, living or dead, actual events, locales or organizations is entirely coincidental.

Copyright © 2017 Book Boyfriends Publishing

All rights reserved. No part of this publication may be reproduced, stored in or introduced into a retrieval system, or transmitted, in any form, or by any means (electronic, mechanical, photocopying, recording, or otherwise) without the prior written permission of the copyright owner. The author acknowledges the trademarked status and trademark owners of various products referenced in this work of fiction, which have been used without permission. The publication/use of the trademarks is not authorized, associated with, or sponsored by the trademark owners.

Table of Contents

Copyright and Disclaimer ii

Chapter 1 7

Chapter 2 13

Chapter 3 29

Chapter 4 51

Chapter 5 81

Chapter 6 99

Chapter 7 127

Chapter 8 139

Chapter 9 155

Chapter 10 169

Chapter 11 191

Chapter 12 201

Chapter 13 221

Chapter 14 233

Chapter 15 245

Chapter 16 263

Chapter 17 269

Chapter 18 277

Chapter 19 287

Chapter 20 301

Beautifully Broken

Reckless Bastards MC

By Wall Street Journal & USA Today Bestselling Author

KB Winters

Chapter 1

Max

"I don't know what you want me to say, Doc. It wasn't even long enough to be a fucking nightmare. I closed my eyes and there I was on the transport vehicle. Seconds later the explosion happened that deafened me and made it damn hard to see. Body parts went flying and then everything went black. I woke up a sweaty and panting mess."

I looked over at Dr. Singh, a tall lanky man with dark brown skin who'd perfected the look of wearing dad sweaters. In the fucking desert.

He nodded, ankle resting on the opposite knee while his hands were clasped on top of his notebook. "Nightmares have no designated length, Max, as I'm sure you know. What did you do after you woke up?"

I couldn't tell him that I'd reached for that hidden bottle of Maker's Mark because he'd already bitched me out about my drinking. "I played some video games and stared at the fucking stars. What else could I do?"

Dr. Singh sighed. "Max, you have to develop healthy coping mechanisms. Having a drink once in a while is fine, but you can't use it to dull the pain or shutdown the memories."

"Yeah, no shit," I smirked and even the Doc couldn't help but join in. "So something other than video games?"

He nodded. "Something outside of your house, maybe, that involves other people. Would that be so terrible?"

Shit. I sat back in the stylish chair in his office that was not meant for a man of my size and sighed. "No, I guess not. But I don't know, shit I haven't done anything for fun in a long damn time."

He nodded and his perfectly styled hair never moved. "How about you go do some things just for fun. Sleep with a pretty lady. Go out for a meal. Vegas is off in the distance and I hear they have some decent restaurants."

I glared at him. "Everyone's a fucking comedian."

Dr. Singh laughed. "The point is, Max, you need to do some things for fun. Not to forget and not to dull the pain. You said you used to draw. Why not sign up for a class?"

"Sign up for a fucking class? No offense, Doc, but I'm a little old for that."

"Not at a college. This is the twenty-first century, Max. There are adult classes, even businesses that cater to this kind of thing. Your job, before our next session, is to go out there and find an art class. Sign up and just fucking do it."

I shrugged, taken aback by hearing his cultured accent say the word fuck. "You got it, Doc." I hated having to see a fucking head shrinker, but Singh seemed to know his shit and he didn't treat me like a fucking head case. "I'll see you next week."

"I look forward to it."

My boots sounded loud on his hard wood floors as I walked out. The lobby was empty, not that I gave a shit, but I didn't have to do that fake smile bullshit people expected. These days I was much better on my own because I was a cranky, miserable bastard. Had been ever since I was medically discharged from the Navy.

I spent nearly all of my adult life in the Navy and most of that as a sniper for the elite SEALs. I loved it, all of it, from recruit training to BUD/S and jump school. It was the most exciting shit I'd ever done and I ate it up, doing good and saving the world, all while being a badass. It meant something to me just like it meant something to all of us. Our unit was family. We'd trained together, fought together, spotted together and killed together. And one damn day in that dirty fucking desert, many of us died together. The problem was only some of us came back.

Sometimes I thought it would've been better if we'd all died out there that day because this life of mine, filled with nightmares and paranoia, was just bullshit. Coming back like this was worse than not coming back at all, because at least if you were dead this shit just stopped. The memories were gone. The pain was gone.

Now though, the pain was constant. Never fucking ending.

The sun helped and every day when I woke up and had coffee out on my deck, I thanked fuck that I'd chosen to come to the desert. Nonstop sun and heat was good for my mental health according to the good doctor, and sun all day made me feel lighter. Freer.

But the sun alone wasn't fucking working so now I had to look for an art class.

Fuck. My. Life.

Chapter 2

Jana

My favorite part of working from home, other than the distinct lack of people, is the fact that I rarely got interrupted. It meant that I could get lost in the structure of accounts and spreadsheets, the tedium and organization of receipts. Accounting wasn't the sexiest job in the world, but it was a necessity. So when the bell rang for the third time, I could no longer pretend to be deaf. "This better be good." As in it better be that old guy with a check for a million dollars or I might scream. I stopped at the door and saw my one and only friend glaring at the peephole.

"Who else would it be, Jana? Let me in!"

Teddy and I couldn't be more different if we tried. Where I was short with more curves than I needed, Teddy was tall and thin with curves *only* in the right places. She was a fiery red to my plain long almost-white blond hair, and her business required her to be out in the thick of things, whereas I'd tailored mine to ensure minimal human contact. But she put up with my grumpy, anti-social ways. To an extent. I shook away all signs of annoyance and opened the door. "Teddy. This is a surprise."

"It is. If I would've called, you'd have been mysteriously absent or come up with a good reason to stay inside. Get dressed girl, we are going out." She rolled her slender hips in a suggestive figure eight that spelled trouble for me.

"What? No." I shook my head, looking at her like she'd grown a second one of her own. "I have to finish these expense reports, plus I'm not ready." Not physically and or mentally, or by any other societal standard. My long blond waves were tied in a knot on top of my head and I wore baggy red cotton pants and an oversized t-shirt from my alma mater, Michigan State. Yeah, it was the only good thing about growing up in foster care, plenty of scholarships for an orphan with perfect grades. "I need time to prepare for that."

"Bullshit. You need to get dressed and make yourself presentable, that's all."

I glared up at her nearly six-foot frame. "Yeah that's kind of the problem, isn't it?"

Teddy rolled her eyes and pushed past me, like I was somehow in the wrong. "Jana, I love you girl, I really, really do. But if you don't get over that slight imperfection on your beautiful face, I'm just going to bash it in." She grinned and flipped her silky red curls over her shoulder. "It's one tiny scar."

"It's six fucking inches!" More like six and three-eighths of an inch if we were going to be exact about it. And it was deep. And jagged. And long, stretching from the corner of my right eye, cutting a pink path straight to the corner of my mouth. It was big and hideous and ugly as fuck. And it was all mine.

Wasn't I a lucky fucking girl?

Teddy stomped her Jimmy Choo's on my hardwood hall like a perturbed child. "Jana, seriously girlfriend, I need you to stop this. It's noticeable, yes.

But it's not hideous. The only reason people notice it is because you make it so damn noticeable."

My hand automatically went to the object of our discussion, touching the offending scar because home was the only place I ever wore my hair up. When I wore it down, hiding the scar was easier. It made my life easier. A lot easier. "It's pretty hard to ignore."

"It is when you're drawing attention to it every five seconds." She whirled on her heels and I had to jog to keep up with her as she made her way to my bedroom. "Go shower. I'll take care of the rest."

I glared up at her for several long minutes, but Teddy was one tough chick. Probably the toughest I'd ever met, which is saying a lot considering I went into foster care when I was eight. But Teddy's tough act wasn't an act to hide a fear or a vulnerability, it was hard earned and impressive to watch. That's how I knew it was a losing battle and my shoulders fell. "Fine." I took a quick shower and blow-dried my hair before reentering the bedroom. "Oh, hell no. Absolutely not!"

"Why not?" She held up a pair of jeans I hadn't worn, or been able to wear, in two years along with a long sleeve tunic that hugged my curves. "This is casual and sexy."

"For starters I can't fit in those jeans."

"Try them." She held them out to me and I snatched them from her, letting the robe fall to the floor and grabbing a pair of black lace panties.

I stepped into the jeans and my stomach tightened. I wasn't one of those girls who constantly worried about what she ate. I ate healthy and turned part of my basement into a gym, but the curves had proven they had more staying power than I did, and all I could do was accept it. So I did. But still, the dark wash denim was at least two sizes too small in the hip and ass area the last time I tried them on. Then something weird happened. They slid up easily over my hips and ass, problem areas all women know well, zipping with the barest hint of resistance. "This doesn't make any sense."

"Sure it does. I told you before that you dropped a few pounds. Are you sure there isn't a man hiding in your love shack out back?"

I rolled my eyes. Teddy was unnaturally curious about my girl cave in the backyard. It had plenty of light from three sides and temperature control but beyond that, it was bare bones. I spent time in there painting and sketching, and I never let anyone inside. Not even Teddy. "It's just art, Teddy."

She huffed. "Right. Finish getting dressed and I'll wait up front."

"Teddy what the hell is going on? We never go out." She knew how much of an ordeal it was for me and usually she didn't push.

"No, we *rarely* go out because you're a pussy and I let you be one, because I'm kind of one too. But not anymore. We're going out to enjoy tacos, nachos, and margaritas. And maybe meet some guys."

I groaned at the last part. I loved Teddy for seeing any beauty in me, but she was my friend. She had no idea what it meant to be disfigured because she was the exact opposite. Beautiful. Perfectly so. The definition of beauty in the world today. Beside her, I only looked worse. "*You* can meet some guys; just be happy I'm going at all."

I didn't bother with any makeup other than a colored gloss as I fluffed big fat curls around my right shoulder. I slid on a pair of strappy heels so I wouldn't look like a child beside her tall frame. "It's not going to get better," I mumbled, spritzed some perfume and took the long, slow walk to the living room.

"Damn girl, you look hot enough to screw."

"I think you're confusing me with your reflection behind me," I deadpanned and grabbed a sweater as I stood near the door. "Ready?"

"Damn straight." She grinned big and put on her best runway walk, the limp that ended her modeling career barely noticeable when she put a little swing in her hips.

***

"I'm so hungry today! I had an early morning Skype meeting with Charlene Simms and I didn't get to eat breakfast." Teddy barely stopped to take a breath as she told me all about the reality songbird with the golden voice. "The girl doesn't know what she wants, no colors or themes or anything. And what she does want," she scoffed, "is the very worst and gaudiest of Vegas styles." I listened to her complain but not really complain. Teddy, an uber successful wedding planner, dealt with difficult clients with more money than sense. It was a stressful job but she loved it.

"I guess it's a good thing she's paying you well."

Teddy's smile lit up her whole face, big ocean blue eyes glittering like jewels. "Very well. It's my favorite part of having rich clientele."

The cute young waitress set down a pitcher of margaritas along with hot tortilla chips and fresh made salsa. I took a sip and listened as Teddy talked gold cummerbunds and top hats for bridesmaids, effortlessly swatting three interested suitors. They were all the same type, the kind of guy way too arrogant to think anyone—never mind one as beautiful as Teddy—could not be interested in them. Thankfully they didn't spare me a look. "You always figure it out," I reassured her because that's all she really wanted.

"It *is* kind of my *thang*," she said, grinning and making her perfect eyebrows dance.

"I would love to be your *thang*," a dark-haired man said as he leaned against the edge of the table, his back to me. Because I'd learned soon after I got the scars, that I was invisible.

I bit back a smile, but Teddy did what beautiful women do in this situation. She laughed. "My plaything or just any old *thang*?"

"Whatever you want, babe."

Her phone rang and vibrated on the table, and Teddy grinned up at him. "What I want is to finish this call so I can finish hanging with my homie. 'Kay?" She patted his shoulder as she slid from the booth, answering the call as she headed toward the door.

I didn't bother looking up, just continued to eat chips and salsa, between sips of strawberry margarita. Teddy was lucky I decided to drive, because these margaritas needed at least two more shots of tequila. I hated being out because people stared. People were cruel and they simply thought it was okay.

"You don't stand a chance with the smokin' redhead, she's got expensive tastes. But take the ugly fat friend, she'll be grateful for a night with a stallion like you, Greg."

The other one, Greg I assumed, laughed with too much energy like he was trying too hard to impress. "She might not be ugly and I don't mind having something to grab on to. Fat chicks love a good hard fuck."

I didn't bother to turn around because I could guess what they looked like. One would have dark hair and the other blond, dressed like some after work office drones. One would probably be better dressed because he made more money, probably *not* Greg. They were both players, probably even had some kind of scoring system for their conquests. *Not* Greg laughed. "Damn man, you're making me want to change my mind about which one I want to stick it to."

I rolled my eyes, grateful when Teddy returned to drown out their asshole bro chatter. "Good news, she's decided on old Hollywood. She's got an audition for some gangster flick set in the twenties and wants these photos to help her land the role." She rolled her eyes and took a long sip from her glass.

We placed our orders and as soon as the waitress rushed off, the two dickheads screwed up their courage and approached our table. The stupidly good looking one, *not* Greg, trained his focus wholly on Teddy while Greg turned to me, practically pinching his nose just to inch closer. "So," he began but I put up a hand to stop him.

"I'll stop you right there, *Greg*, the fat ugly chick isn't interested a good hard fuck with your tiny limp dick. Go back to the bar and wait for your *bro* to strike out with the hot one."

He looked at me, eyes flashed surprise for a moment and then anger. "Whatever."

"Oooh, good comeback," I scoffed and rolled my eyes before returning to my margarita. I might not be much to look at but even with the scar I was average looking. I knew my strengths and weaknesses and one day I might find someone who could tell them apart. Until then, it was just me.

Not Greg continued to lay down every cheesy pickup line and compliment he downloaded from some pickup artist website, while I dug into my fish tacos. Teddy looked longingly at her spicy beef nachos while *Todd*—because *of course,* Todd—did his best impression of the hot jerk from every teen movie and soap ever created.

Finally, she called time of death. She turned her big blue eyes up to him, just a hint of a smile in them and flicked her hair off her shoulders. "Todd I'm going to be honest with you because you are seriously hot and

I think we have a connection." It was a total lie, but it was part one of her best letdown. "I'm not looking for casual sex. I want a husband and kids and I plan to have both within the next eighteen months. I'm not sure that's what you're looking for, is it?"

This was my favorite part. Where he tried to figure out how to best lie without just telling her what she wanted to hear. He wanted to just say that's what he wanted too, because he was that kind of guy, but he probably sensed Teddy would be able to tell if he was lying. "I'm not opposed to all that, I mean, it's all part of the plan, right?" He flashed a charming grin that probably got him out of all kinds of trouble.

"Eventually."

His shoulders fell and he walked away without a goodbye.

"You enjoyed that," I accused.

"Maybe, but he deserved it."

"No way, if you're interested go after him. Don't let me stop you."

"If this wasn't so good, I would throw it at you," she pointed at a nacho before tossing it in her mouth. "I know you don't believe this, but it's kind of the girl code. If a guy doesn't like your best friend, he's toast."

I swallowed and tried to ignore the warmth that spread through me at hearing her call me her best friend. We were friends, sure, but I assumed she had other friends she shared things with or went on shopping trips with in those fancy casino shops. "Oh."

She laughed. "You know what I love about you Jana, you're like a robot with your big brain and super observation skills. I feel like I'm teaching you about regular humans."

I smiled because I knew she meant it as a compliment. "I'm saying thank you only because you're my friend." My best friend, apparently. We finished our food and paid the bill, but as we were leaving I felt a prickle of awareness, of being watched wash over me. I'd felt that feeling once before and I'd reacted too late to save myself a lifetime of heartache and a world of pain.

I scanned the restaurant but I didn't see any faces I recognized, not that I would. I ran far from my last foster home in Detroit and changed my name so that when he got out, the bastard who did this to me could never find me.

I picked up the speed and hauled ass to Teddy's fancy ass Benz she insisted I drive. I did love the cool gadgets though, so I only put up a token protest before driving us back to my place.

KB Winters

Chapter 3

Max

"He thinks taking an art class will help. Why can't I just paint in my own damn yard?" Carl Brandt was my commanding officer for years and a good friend even longer, and right now he was my sounding board.

"Man up, Ellison. You can take off a man's skull at a thousand yards, you can damn well go and paint some fruit in the desert." He also didn't ever pull a fucking punch, no matter how much I wished he would. He didn't sugarcoat or coddle.

"Just like that?"

"Hell, yes," he grumbled, voice thick like a man who indulged in expensive cigars a little too often. "One of these days Max, you're gonna want to get laid again, or maybe make some little frogs for me to command. To do that, you'll need to get your head on straight. If painting gets you there, do it."

I nodded even though he couldn't see me, because I guessed I just wanted someone I respected to tell me what I'd been thinking. "Thank you, sir. Class starts in an hour."

His deep thunderous laugh sounded down the line and I couldn't help but smile. "Sounds like you're ready." He let his words hang in the air for a minute and I soaked them in. Could it really be as simple as being ready to be better? "Any word on your brother?"

I sighed. "No. Tate wrote me about six months ago, saying there might be some new evidence in his case but he won't call me back or see me when I go visit him." It gutted me to have my baby brother locked up for a crime he didn't commit. But I'd hired everyone I could to help get him out and now he'd shut me out. I wanted to help but he was a man, and if he felt the need to fight this battle on his own, I had to let him. Even if it killed me.

"My wife keeps him in her prayers, son. Six years is a long time to spend in prison in general, but especially for another man's crimes. Want me to see if I can find out anything?"

"If you wouldn't mind, it's just I can't have both things weighing on me."

"Then you won't have to. Go to your class. Flirt with a pretty girl and paint something nice. Talk soon." He disconnected the call before I could express even more gratitude.

With a shrug, I stood and scanned the living room since it was time to go. I stared at my *kutte* for a long minute, unsure if I wanted to wear it. In the end, I opted not to wear it, not because I was ashamed of my club. I wasn't. Reckless Bastards MC saved me when I needed it.

Two years ago, I was fresh out of the SEALs and my mind was all fucked up, and all I wanted to do was come see my baby brother. Only to find out he was in jail. No, not jail, fucking prison, and he'd already been there for years. But his club took me in, kept me safe when my mind would have me hurt myself and others.

They treated me as one of their own, and eventually I was.

But lately, sleepless nights and a restless mind had made me a shit member. Between Tate and my own fucked up head, I didn't have time for club business. The Reckless Bastards weren't like other clubs. We kicked ass only when we needed to, and we didn't fuck with any drugs except weed. Tourists came here for it now and they loved buying legal weed from big ass bikers, and they loved it even more that the town was called Mayhem. Because of the pot and the custom bike work, we didn't need to fuck with guns or hard drugs, instead the third leg of club business was ass. Titty bars and brothels for every income bracket, legal in Nevada, and it was more than enough to keep us flush.

But still, I knew I hadn't been carrying my weight at the club. Hopefully this painting class tonight would help with that.

The little storefront in the middle of the street looked girly and expensive, the oversized windows featuring pricey paintbrushes and easels. Inside was more relaxed, with soft muted colors surrounding all the materials. "Just go straight on to the back," a voice called from somewhere to my left.

"Okay, thanks." I did as the voice said and went down a dark hall that opened into a spacious room with paint-splattered floors. Nearly a dozen chairs and easels sat in a half circle and only one other person had arrived, a woman with long white-blond hair sat at the chair all the way on the right with her head down as she arranged her palette. I could have taken any seat, but I took the one right beside her.

She didn't turn or acknowledge me at all, so I sat there and looked around, until the teacher came in, a graceful woman with long black hair streaked with silver. She wore a billowing red dress that looked to be made of rayon or some other crinkly material and nearly two dozen bracelets covered her arms. She gave me a strange look, shrugged and went back to setting up her own easel plus the wooden crate in the center of the half circle.

"Hi," I leaned over and whispered.

"Hi," she said softly. Her voice was smooth and gentle.

"We don't get graded or anything, do we?" I didn't look over because she kept her head down, clearly not wanting me to look at her. Or see something, I hadn't decided yet.

"No. Just a chance to paint. And socialize."

I opened my mouth to ask her name when several women stomped in on pointy heels, carrying two bottles of wine each, and wearing sashes. One wore a tiara that said 'bachelorette'. "Shit. A bachelorette party." A snicker sounded at my right and I grinned. "I'm glad my pain amuses you."

She laughed again and I realized her voice was deeper, huskier, than it seemed at first. She had the voice of a woman. "Sorry. Incoming," she whispered and quickly turned away. I swore I heard a squeak but her warning had me on edge.

I looked up to see one of the women sauntering my way, a little wobbly on her stilts. "Hello, handsome."

"Uh, hi." Everything about her screamed 'woman on the prowl' from her skintight jeans to her low cut top that showed everything but the nipple.

"Why don't you come sit with us?" She leaned over, giving me an even bigger eyeful of round pale tits. She squeezed my arm.

I wasn't going anywhere. I glanced over my shoulder and leaned forward. "I would, but this is part of our date night and my girl is crazy jealous." I thumbed toward the blond beside me. "So you should probably join your friends."

She glanced over my shoulder and I have no idea what she saw, or if she saw anything but a golden curtain of hair, but she huffed, turned and walked off with plenty of swing in her hips. "He's got a jealous girlfriend so he's a no go," she shouted to the rest of her friends. They all groaned their disappointment.

"Thanks," I whispered. She shrugged and I turned to look at her, what I could see, anyway. She was pretty; her lips were plump and pink, with just a hint of moisture on them. But her cheekbone was high and sharp, like a warrior princess. I couldn't see much else because her hair hung nearly to her waist in thick wavy tendrils.

The teacher stepped in front of the class, did her spiel and then we all got down to work to paint the fruit, cheeseboard and a decanter half filled with red wine sitting beside the bottle. "Shit." I mostly drew landscapes and the sky, nothing like this.

"Just focus on what you can draw first."

I grunted. "I don't see any trees or an ocean."

She laughed. "Try the cheeseboard. Focus on the detail in the wood grain of the board."

I looked at it again for a long time, taking in the multiple shades of brown and the small crack between the Gouda and the Brie. "Yeah, I can do that. Thanks."

"No problem." She spoke so quietly I had to lean closer just to hear her. I didn't think it was a power play though, I suspected she was shy. Or scared. Maybe both.

"You're very chatty," I told her.

She didn't speak for so long I thought maybe she wouldn't. "I get that a lot. My best friend can never get a word in."

I laughed. I actually laughed at her deadpan delivery, and damn it felt so damn good to laugh. "Thank you."

"For what?" She seemed baffled.

"I can't remember the last time I laughed." I don't know why I shared that with her, but it was true.

"No kidding," she added with a healthy dose of commiseration before her hand began to move again. She flicked her wrist in quick, sure strokes, her face a study in concentration so I turned back to my own easel and focused on the damn cheeseboard. What the hell was a cheeseboard, anyway? They couldn't have used plates like everyone else?

But after a while it started to look like what it was. Mostly.

"Okay ladies and gentleman, thank you for a great night of painting." The teacher walked around the room but the bachelorettes were quickly wobbling towards the exit. "Not bad, Mr....?"

"Call me, Max. I've never done anything but landscapes. Seascapes and a few of the sky. This is ... different."

She smiled and laid a kind hand on my shoulder. "You did well, I love the grain you brought to life. I can almost smell the cheese." She looked so genuine I had to believe her, but to me it looked like shit.

"Well, thanks, I'm not sure what else I could have painted."

She nodded and stepped over to the mysterious blond. "Oh Jana, it's wonderful. It's somber somehow, like this is set out for a sad event."

"Thanks," she replied on a sigh that didn't sound at all like she liked what she heard. "I'll see you next week, Moon."

Moon? I didn't even want to think about that, so I separated the brushes and stuck the palette in the bucket of warm water and followed Jana out. "Thanks for your help in there. And the laugh."

"No worries," she said, glancing over so once again I only got a view of her left side. "Have a good night, Max."

"You too, Jana." I stood on the sidewalk for way longer than I probably should have, watching the graceful move of her hips, her legs. The swell of her ass. She was beautiful from what I could see, and guarded as hell.

And I would see her again. Next week.

***

"So, it helped?" Dr. Singh sat back in his chair, legs crossed at the knee with a smug smile on his face.

I shrugged. "I still didn't sleep for shit, but it was more of a restless sleep. The dream was still there but it was fuzzy. Mostly just sounds." Two shots of Maker's Mark would have cleared that shit right up, but for some reason I decided to abstain.

"But that's still good after one class. I suspect there is more."

I hadn't planned to talk about Jana at all. I wanted to keep it to myself for just a little while, which was crazy as fuck because there was jack shit to keep to myself. But who the hell else would I talk about it to? "Her name is Jana. She's curvy as hell, like a woman should be. Pretty from what I could see and shy. But she's also hiding something."

"Aren't we all?" he asked, leaning back now that the story was over.

"Like a black eye or something, Doc, not a deep dark secret or a man locked in the basement. You sure you didn't serve?"

He grinned. "No, but I *have* spent my career studying and helping service members and law enforcement deal with the effects and demands of their jobs." He gave me an amused look and I just rolled my eyes. "You like her."

"I don't know her, but I am intrigued." And that was the kicker because as a rule, women didn't intrigue me. They always had their motivations and the only thing I ever appreciated was the chase. And the first fuck, nothing is as good as that first fuck.

"Intrigued is good. Pursue it."

I laughed. "You matchmaking now, Doc?"

He fought the grin, but the battle was lost. "If you need me to, but it doesn't have to be romantic. You could start as friends, or maybe an art buddy."

An art buddy? I laughed. "That's the second time I laughed this week." It still felt weird, but a good kind of weird.

"Good. Keep it up. Are you going to class again?"

"Yeah." The painting was nice and it was better than sitting at home doing nothing, or going to the clubhouse to drink and dick around.

Dr. Singh stood and extended an arm, sinewy with muscle. "I look forward to hearing all about it. How's the drinking?"

"Here and there, mostly beer."

"Good. I'll see you next week, Max."

"Later, Doc." I waved and made my way out into the damn near sweltering early afternoon. I loved the desert air, but goddamn these days felt almost as bad as the other fucking desert. Still, it was early and I didn't have much to do today so I decided to go for a walk around Mayhem. It had been a while since I'd just gone for a walk.

Mayhem was a small desert town, but it wasn't isolated and desolate like so many towns in the state. Vegas was fifteen miles away and when the sun went down, the only thing that could be seen were those familiar bright lights. But Mayhem, despite its name, was a thriving small town with an old west feel.

Tourists loved the wooden sidewalks on Main Street, and the red, white & blue awnings that were straight out of the seventies, and the fact that we had those old school lampposts. Mayhem even had a fucking General Store. Right beside the Bud Café, owned and operated by the Reckless Bastards. It was a cute little town, which was why we worked hard to keep it clean and to keep our businesses on the right side of the law.

I turned the corner into the small park that had been dedicated to the town by an old resident who'd gone on to be somebody big, apparently. I spotted a figure in the distance, wearing a pretty green and white polka dot dress with her legs crossed all proper. The closer I got, the more details became clear. She was sketching something, her face parallel with the pad, long blonde hair covering her shoulders and most of the pad.

She was so engrossed in her sketching, wrist flicking quickly and efficiently, she didn't look up when I approached her or when I stepped behind her to see what she worked on. It was a face, or more accurately it was a set of eyes. Hard and intense, and filled with pain. Finally, Jana froze and turned slowly until big, elliptical brown eyes stared up at me, angry and wary. "Excuse me."

"It *is* you," I said lamely. "It's me, Max."

"I remember," she said cautiously and inched away, closing her sketchpad and shoving it into her hobo style bag. "Did you need help with something?"

"Nah," I shoved my hands into my pockets and grinned. "I thought it was you from a distance, and I just wanted to say hi. You're pretty good at sketching too."

"I do okay," she muttered, head down, keeping the right side of her face away from me.

I didn't like that she seemed afraid of me. "You scared of me, honey?" It'd been a while since a woman was afraid of me, but with the tattoos and the bike, sometimes it happened.

Jana jerked upright and frowned at me. "What? Why would I be afraid of you, more importantly should I be?"

I bit back a grin. "Hell no, you shouldn't. I'm harmless."

She scoffed. "Somehow I doubt that." She closed the flap on her bag and stood, taking a step back.

"So you just don't like me? You're not attracted to me?"

She sighed, clearly becoming frustrated with my interference. "I don't know you to like or dislike you."

"But you're attracted to me, and that's a start. Have lunch with me." Sparring verbally with Jana was the most fun I'd had in a long time.

I watched her carefully. She sucked in a deep breath and let it out slowly, and did it again. Then again. She seemed to brace herself for something, tucking her hair behind her right ear and looking up at me so that I could see what she was hiding. A long, nasty scar from her right eye to the corner of her mouth. It was red and it looked painful, but it wasn't the most interesting thing about her face. Her lips and cheeks were tied for first in that area. "Happy now?"

I stood and stared at her for a long time, taking in her defensive posture as she began to squirm. I grinned. "Is that supposed to scare me?" I let out a laugh that wasn't amused at all as I lifted my shirt and tilted to the left. "A fucking kid snuck up on me in my nest and shoved it straight through my gut, and this ain't the worst of it." I let the shirt drop and crossed my arms, noting the way her gaze tracked over my arms and hands. "I'm sure what happened to you was fucking awful, but a tiny little scar doesn't scare me. Now, can we go eat or do you want to see another one?"

She stared at me for a long time and I thought she'd smack me or tell me to fuck off. But she didn't, and soon I found myself exploring her ripe feminine curves. The jeans she wore did very good things for her hips and shapely thighs, even if she did try and hide what looked like a spectacular rack underneath an oversized t-shirt. Finally, she spoke. "Are there many more scars?"

I blinked until my brows dipped low. "What?"

"The scars, I'm curious how many you have." She didn't wear a smile that said she was flirting or kidding, she looked serious.

"Too many to count. Why, you interested?"

She shrugged and my cock sprang to life. "Between the muscles and the tattoos, I think I might like to get you down on paper, so I'm curious if you have more texture than just muscles and ink."

I grinned at her words. She was quiet, but not shy at all. "You can even have me on sheets. Or carpet, or sofa cushions." I laughed when she rolled her eyes and a smile curled her plump lips.

"You like Greek food?"

I shrugged. "Don't know. Never had it."

"Lamb and potatoes? Yogurt and lemon?"

I didn't really give a damn as long as we could sit and talk. I wanted to get to know Jana.

"You're staring."

"Sorry, it's just—"

"It's hard not to look at?"

What? "You're nuts. No, I'm just glad you weren't hiding a black eye under all that damn hair." That sounded a bit grumpier than I wanted it to, but she just grinned. "I might like Greek. Want to get on my bike?"

"No thanks. I like my brains in my head. You can follow me. I'm the green Subaru over there."

"You're not what I thought you'd be," I told her as I fell in step beside her. Okay, a little behind her because damn that heart-shaped ass was the kind that made men lose their minds.

"How did you think I'd be?"

There was a landmine if I ever encountered one, and a smarter man would dodge. "I thought you were shy until a few minutes ago, but I like this sassy, smart ass version of you."

She stopped at her car, shoving the key in and tossing her bag on the passenger seat. "I am shy. Unless strange men sneak up on me and invade my personal space."

I grinned again and held her door open for her. "Noted. I'm a few blocks up that way."

"Get in, I'll take you."

"You will?"

"I will," she nodded. "Unless you prefer that I drive slowly alongside you like a creeper."

I laughed and scratched my chin. "I don't know, I've never had a stalker before."

"It's not all it's cracked up to be," she mumbled and put the car in drive as soon as my ass hit the seat. I realized that must be a sensitive topic and now that I saw the scar, I had a new batch of questions for the intriguing girl with the sinful curves.

Chapter 4

Jana

"How about the number one, five and nine to start?" I knew Max was unfamiliar with Greek food, but I assumed based on his tattoos and his motorcycle that he was a bit of a risk taker.

But he looked at the menu with a deep frown on his face. "Octopus?"

I couldn't help but laugh at him. "Don't tell me such a tough guy is afraid of a little octopus?" At his affronted look I laughed even more. "I'm ordering it because I love it, but I think you should at least taste it."

He stared at me for a long time and I found myself turning away so my scar was less visible, but his gaze didn't waver because he was focused on my mouth. "Okay."

And that was it. Just okay. "Why are you taking art classes, Max?" He seemed to have some artistic skill, but his discomfort last week had been apparent.

He sighed and the look in his gray eyes darkened to a gunmetal color as his entire demeanor changed. A big hand slid through short black hair and he leaned back. "Can I get away with saying that I like art?"

"Sure. Your secrets are your own. Do you draw at home?"

"Not for a while, no. Maybe I should. How about you, why do you take the class?"

"It gets me out of my house and I get a chance to improve my skill with Moon's help." I started taking the art classes about six months ago as I started to experiment beyond drawing and painting.

"So, are you some kind of artist?"

I shook my head even though the more I looked at him, the more my fingers itched to draw him. Paint him. Put him down on paper for future civilizations to discover. "Nope, it's strictly a hobby."

The waiter stopped and flashed me a grin as he set down our starters and drinks. "Maybe it shouldn't be. You're damn good, Jana."

I felt my skin heat up from his compliment. "Thanks." Other than Teddy and my satisfied clients, I didn't hear many compliments and I was all right with that. I didn't need accolades for my looks or my work, but it was nice to hear once in a while. "You're not bad either, but you'd be better if you believed in yourself. As cliché as that sounds."

His deep laugh sounded rich and multi-layered in the near empty restaurant. It was a bit rusty, paying truth to his words last week that he hadn't laughed in a while. "When I first got out of the service I … struggled. I couldn't sleep most nights, so I'd go out and paint, wherever I was. The desert, the forest, lakes and rivers, oceans and everything in between."

"So you don't have much practice painting anything else?" He nodded, and I felt an answering grin tug on my lips. "I know how that is. I first started painting and sketching. Self-portraits. You wouldn't believe how quickly I got over them."

His grin deepened and I swallowed. Hard. Max was too much man, far too big and muscular, and he had that rugged handsome thing going on that definitely spelled danger to a woman like me. Guys like him didn't go for girls like me. They'd pretended in college to get my help with papers and homework, only to drop the pretense immediately after. And when I graduated and worked at a large accounting firm, a few guys had tried to get me to do their reports with the vague promise of a date in the future. I learned my lesson quickly and stayed far, far away from men. All men.

He gave me a grin I couldn't interpret. "I can only imagine."

I looked away for a moment, then asked, "What branch of the military did you serve?"

Again, his gray eyes took on that cold, haunted look. "Navy. I was a SEAL." He braced himself and I knew what he was waiting for because I'd seen the way women got all giddy with stars in their eyes at Navy SEALs, and I can only imagine how crazy they went over a guy like Max.

"Thank you for your service. Before...everything, did you feel fulfilled by it?"

He blinked and thought about it as I sliced the octopus, offering him a few pieces along with the garlic and herb butter.

"I never thought about it like that, but yeah, I was. Shit, maybe that's why it's been so hard." He stabbed the slice of meat with more force than necessary and slid it off the fork into his mouth. "Fuck me, that's a tender piece of meat. And this is octopus?"

"It is," I told him and sliced a few pieces for myself and pushed the plate to the middle of the table. "Why did you retire?" He frowned and I held up a hand. "I meant, isn't it common for hardcore Navy guys like you to teach and pass on the knowledge?"

Max nodded and my gaze was riveted to his steely gray eyes. They should've been intimidating with that thousand-yard stare, but they were compelling. Too damn compelling. "Yeah, but it wasn't a right fit for me."

My heart went out to Max because of all the women he could have possibly met, I knew exactly what he was going through. "It takes time." We fell silent and finished the starters before we both decided to order a beer. "Where are you from, Max?"

"Brooklyn originally, but I haven't lived there since I was eighteen." He chuckled good-naturedly. "A lifetime ago. What about you?"

I shrugged. "Detroit, I think." It had been a long time since someone showed an interest in my life and I was a bit rusty. "I went into the foster care system in Michigan when I was six so it's a bit fuzzy before that, but I bounced around plenty of Detroit foster homes, so let's go with that. Siblings?"

He grinned and holy shit, his face was transformed from a ruggedly handsome warrior to a boyishly charming man far too good-looking for my peace of mind. "I have a brother and we were close. It was just me and him and our mom, at least until I went into the Navy. He went Army as soon as he was old enough, but Tate didn't make a career of it."

I swallowed. "Did he die?" I couldn't take it if a man like him, who had sacrificed for our country, had experienced that kind of loss. It didn't seem fair or right, two things I knew life didn't guarantee.

"No."

"Oh. Good." He apparently didn't want to talk about it so I dropped it. Teddy often said I had a bad habit of being too nosy.

"Sorry, it's just. My brother is going through some shit right now and I want to help but he's shutting me out." He blew out a long breath and fell against the seat.

"You can't take it personally, Max."

"He's my damn brother! My only family."

"He's lucky to have you, but sometimes shit is so hard, so painful that the only thing you can do is curl into yourself and handle it the best way you know how." The brothers had no idea how lucky they were to have each other, but telling Max that wouldn't help. "So, what do you do now?"

"Depends on what the club needs. I got a business degree while I was in the military so mostly I take care of the business end of club business."

He'd said that world, club, a few times since we sat down and I understood. "Motorcycle club?"

Tension curled through the hard muscles of his shoulders and arms. Everything about him was so tense suddenly, like he was worried I'd judge him. "Yep."

He didn't need to worry because I didn't judge. Ever. "Like an outlaw biker club with one percenters? Or are you a bunch of nine to fivers who ride as weekend warriors?" I'd recently binge watched *Sons of Anarchy* and had thirsted for all things biker related.

He laughed. "We're not outlaws but we're not nine to fivers. Our businesses are legal but we're like a brotherhood. They helped keep me and the public safe when I first landed here looking for Tate."

"That's nice of them. Do you all have to ride Harley's? Oh, are all of you white or former military?"

He grinned. "You ask a lot of questions, you know that?"

"I don't get out a lot and I rarely meet anyone with so much life experience. I'm curious." I couldn't stop staring at him any more than I could resist the urge to turn so only the left side of my face was visible.

His facial features were strong, a sharp, jawline and a nose that looked like it had been broken a few times only made him look more well-lived. Miles of skin that included scars, tattoos, too much sun, all signs he hadn't wasted the life he was given. Max was way out of my league, but I liked talking to him. "You can tell me it's none of my business. I won't be offended."

"We don't have stupid ass rules about race. Most of us have served in the military at some point and that brotherhood means a hell of a lot more than the color of our skin."

"Do you have any members who can't ride motorcycles?"

He grinned. "A few old timers who mostly sit around the clubhouse and take care of our business interests."

"Wow. You are an interesting man, Max."

"Ellison. Max Ellison."

I smiled. "Jana Carter. Nice to meet you. Officially." He smiled and my heart sped up, pounding so hard I thought it might crack a rib just to get out. "You're not going to ask about my face?" Most people, especially kids, old people and men, wanted to know right up front.

"I'm curious but I figured if you wanted me to know, you'd tell me."

Damn. "I appreciate that, but it's always the elephant in the room. The short version is that my foster dad did it to me."

His jaw clenched and this time his gaze did linger on the scar and I felt my stomach flip with nausea. I hated that fucking scar, so red and painful and ugly. "It's not as noticeable as you think, but please tell me the prick is in prison."

"He is. For now." I didn't know how to feel about someone being so upset on my behalf. Even when it happened, no one gave a damn. Not the police or social services, and certainly not the one woman I thought actually loved me.

"Good. Now tell me Jana Carter, what do you do for fun?"

I laughed at his unexpected topic change. "I cook, watch documentaries on just about everything and I paint. Occasionally my friend Teddy forces me out into the world." My smile dimmed as I thought about Todd and Greg. "But I prefer to stay home."

A flash of something, sympathy or commiseration maybe, showed in his gray eyes but it disappeared so fast I figured it was wishful thinking. "Good to know. Can I call you sometime, Jana?"

Yes. "Why?"

He frowned. "What kind of question is that?"

I didn't want to get into this after we had such a nice meal, but I found it was better to get this part out of the way sooner rather than later. Not that I'd even been this far with a man since sophomore year of college when I learned a lesson I never forgot. "It's a perfectly valid one. Look at me Max, guys like you don't want to spend time with me or hang out with me unless you need something. I work for myself so unless you need accounting help, that's not it. Teddy," I said as realization dawned. "You want me to introduce you to her?" It wouldn't be the first time. Or the last.

"Who the fuck is Teddy and why would I want to meet her when you're right here?"

"I uh, I'm not...shit." I finger combed my hair down so it covered the right side of my face. "I don't know how to answer that."

He frowned but slowly, it turned into a smile. "Jana, you intrigue me. You're beautiful even though you can't see it, and your body is hot as sin. I'd like to get to know you better, spend some time with you. Is that so hard to believe?"

"It is," I told him honestly. "But I've had a good time today talking with you." I handed him my phone and he did the same. "Please don't make me regret it."

Max paid the bill and walked me to my car as the sun began her journey to the other side of the world. "I've had a good time today, Jana. Thank you." He leaned forward and I froze. Was he going to kiss me? I hadn't been kissed in years and I was completely unprepared. Were my lips chapped? Did I have octopus breath?

I had no reason to worry though, his surprisingly soft lips landed on my cheek, a breath away from the corner of my mouth. "Max," I whispered.

"I'll talk to you soon, Jana."

Why that gave me shivers, I couldn't say.

***

Tonight's class featured a nude model. A nude male model, but for the sake of propriety a colorful scarf had been draped over his hips to cover the man meat. Thank goodness because tonight, Max and I were joined by eight women in their forties pretending to be a book club.

"Oh Moon, you spoil us, sweetheart!"

I kept quiet, my gaze on my station, prepping my palette and canvas. Max had yet to arrive, but class didn't start for another seven minutes. Not that I was worried. I wasn't. Late lunch with him had been nice on Wednesday but I hadn't heard from him, so I decided not to worry about it. Or think about it. I'd never had a man in my life, so I couldn't really miss what I didn't have.

Moon gave a kind smile. "You ladies just got lucky tonight. Don't mind them, Kyle."

Kyle wore a faint shade of pink all over, but he flashed a dimpled smile at the ladies and sent them into a fit of giggles more appropriate for a fifth-grade slumber party. I rolled my eyes and kept my gaze averted. I learned not long after leaving the hospital with my scars, that eye contact made people want to interact. Ask questions.

Fuck that.

"Oh, hello handsome. You are just what mama needs."

I knew before looking up that Max had arrived. Not only because of the catcalling women, but because the air changed. It was electrified and thick.

I was too aware of him and in protest, I refused to look his way. Not until he took the seat beside me, the air from his movement blowing tendrils of my hair. "Hey Jana." Even his voice had a smile in it.

"Hey."

"How's it going?"

"It's going. You?" There was no reason to hold a grudge because he didn't call. I didn't really think he would, even if a tiny sliver of me wished he had.

"All right," he said but his words were heavy. Anxious.

"You sure about that?" I swiveled in my chair and looked at him. I really looked at him and he was tense all over.

"Not even a little bit, Jana."

I gave him a sympathetic smile and patted his shoulder. "Want to get lost in some painting?"

He looked to Kyle's nearly nude form and back to me, one brow quirked up in a gesture that clearly said, "Get real." I laughed. "Yeah I guess."

That's what we did. I focused on the curve of Kyle's hip leading to his thigh because he was a beautiful picture of masculinity. And because I never got a chance to see a man this delicious up close. A quick glance at Max's canvas showed he focused on the bicep, and he did a pretty good job.

The book club women were loud and boisterous, but they were having a good time and I envied that. Though I always felt a certain peace when I painted, I envied the good time they had together, laughing and drinking. So free and sure of their friendships. When class was over, I let out an exhausted breath and stood, stretching with my back facing the class.

"You mad at me?"

I froze and looked over my left shoulder. "No, why would I be?"

"I said I would call and I didn't."

I knew he was a nice guy. "Don't worry about it; I didn't really think you would. No harm, no foul."

He sighed and touched my shoulder, but he didn't do anything to move me so I turned to face him. "Jana, shit. I had a really good time the other day and I went to bed and slept. Like I haven't slept in a long damn time. But the next night, I felt guilty as hell about it and I slept for shit."

"I'm sorry to hear that, Max. Want to grab a drink and tell me about it?" Where in the hell did that come from? I never extended offers to hang out with anyone.

Not even Teddy, really. Unless it was at my house, or sometimes hers.

He looked as surprised as I felt. "Really? Because I thought you were pissed off."

"I was annoyed but mostly with myself for thinking you'd call. And I can't believe I said that out loud." He chuckled and I felt slightly less embarrassed.

"Yeah, I think we do need to have a drink and talk. About a few things." His gaze was determined and a chill shot through me at the intensity in his gaze. "Where to?"

"Follow me." I didn't feel like going to a bar, especially with a guy like Max. Everyone would stare and wonder why he was with me and I just didn't feel like dealing with that tonight. Besides, I figured Max wanted to talk in private and my backyard was the perfect location.

It took the entire drive home to get my nerves under control. This was nothing but a platonic talk with a guy I'd met; it didn't have to be anything more than that. I knew that, even if my silly heart wanted it to be more. I pulled into my driveway and his bike came to a stop beside me. He pulled my door open. "Never heard of this place before."

"Funny. This is my place. I figured we could use the privacy for our chat." He gave me a funny look that made me smile. "Only to chat. Believe me, even if I wanted to, I wouldn't know where to begin seducing a guy like you."

He laughed. "Sweetheart, I'm halfway to seduced just looking at the way you fill out your jeans."

Well, shit. I felt my cheeks flush. "See, *that*! I wish I could just say something smooth like that. Damn."

I fanned myself and nodded for him to follow me. His chuckle sounded behind me and I was happy I wore my hair down so he couldn't see my flushed skin. I kicked my shoes off and turned on the lights, trying hard not to think about what he thought of my place. It was decorated to suit me, comfortable and attractive. In the middle of the desert, my little place was country chic.

"Nice place. It's very you."

"Rustic?"

He laughed. "No. Understated—but nice to look at."

"Ohhh, you're good." I was nervous but I walked through to the kitchen and flipped on the lights. "Tequila work for you?" I turned to face him, and dammit, again I was struck by just how handsome he was. He shouldn't be, not with that perma-scowl on his face, but there was something about him that had my body acting like a dog in heat.

"Hell yeah it works."

I grinned, pulling out two limes and slicing them onto a plate. I handed him a couple bottles of water and we went out to my yard. We sat in companionable silence for a while, both of us lost in our own thoughts.

"This is nice," he said finally from the lounger to my right. Both of them were covered in paisley cushions with a table between them and about five feet away was a fire pit for when the desert nights turned chilly.

"Thanks." I didn't know if he would just start talking, or if he expected me to pull the info from him, so I poured two shots and sipped mine.

"I lost half my crew. We were on our way back from a mission and it was what it always fucking was, a damn roadside bomb. It was loud and I couldn't see. All I could hear was the sounds of my brothers screaming in pain and gunshots. I got behind what was left of the transport vehicle and shot. I shot until I ran out of ammo and then I grabbed weapons off disembodied limbs and kept shooting until someone came to save the three of us who remained." He laughed bitterly, shaking his head, looking handsome in his moonlight anguish. "They gave me fucking medals for that shit, Jana. And I can't stop thinking about it."

I could hear the pain in his voice. "Tell me about them."

"Who," he barked out, frowning at me.

"The guys. Your brothers."

"Why?"

I bit back a smile. "You're very monosyllabic tonight. Because I'd like to know a little about the men who died to keep me safe." That took all the wind out of his sails and he snatched the shot glass off the table, throwing the smooth tequila back like a pro.

He smiled as the memories came to him. "Jameson loved the Bulls. He grew up during the Jordan-Pippen-Rodman era and I swear that kid could tell you every moment of every game played. Garcia was first generation American but man he was proud of being Mexican. His *abuela* sent the best fucking salsa you've ever had. He made us all learn that Spanish Christmas song too," he laughed, and this time it was just a huff of amusement, but it was peaceful. "Reilly was a cowboy, from a big ass ranch in Texas and he would always talk about his favorite spot to sweet talk the ladies, overlooking a field of brown eyed Susan's. Never even heard of them before him, but now I'll never forget."

I poured another shot into the empty glass he held, earning a grateful smile. "They sound like amazing men."

"They were just my brothers. We all had a job to do and we did it as best as we could."

"I'm glad you made it back."

"Thanks," he huffed out and leaned back, turning his gaze up to the stars. "What's your favorite song?"

I laughed. "Free Bird. Yours?"

"Don't have one."

"Everyone has a favorite song."

"I was out of the country for most of the last two decades, darlin'."

"Right. Well then how about I put on some songs, jog your memory?" I opened a music app on my phone and let it play.

"I wouldn't have pegged you as a classic rock girl."

I shrugged, even though he couldn't see me, and I slid off my chair stretched out in the small patch of grass that was my lawn, staring up at the night sky. "One of the first things I ever got that was mine, which was almost never, was a portable CD player. My caseworker got it for me when I won the gold for Mathletes. It was used and there was one of those best of CD's and it was classic rock. I loved it. It was gritty and it made me smile and I was hooked."

Max curled down beside me and turned to me, his gaze intense. On my right side. "Play some." I did, starting with Free Bird. We let it play all the way through, but it was a live version, so it was long, but I figured Max needed it. I don't imagine it was easy talking about his friends, but I knew how much it could help.

"I like it. My ma used to listen to this. She loved Joni Mitchell and Fleetwood Mac."

I grinned. "Landslide and Rhiannon are on my gardening playlist."

"How'd you end up an accountant in Nevada?"

I sighed, and sat up to pour another shot for both of us. "Cheers." We clinked our glasses and I threw back the alcohol and let the liquid slide down my throat.

"My last foster family, Robert and Karen Sanborn, were mostly good people. I thought Karen loved me. I'd been with them since I was twelve. But her husband Robert was a pervert. As soon as I turned sixteen, he started to follow me with his eyes and then literally. Then he tried to sneak into my room, but I would scream or knock things over because I knew Karen would come running." She'd been the closest thing to a mother I could remember but it was all tainted by what came next.

"I had a job doing data entry part-time because a lot of companies were working toward going digital and I worked fast and away from people. It was my last year of high school so I only attended half a day, coming home to change into business clothes for work."

I sighed and reached to pick up the bottle but Max's big warm hand wrapped around mine. He held it within his and dropped into the soft grass. "Robert was waiting for me that day. Karen wouldn't be home for hours and it was the perfect time for him to get what he wanted. He stripped me down, cutting my school clothes off, my favorite Jim Morrison t-shirt. Anyway, there I was, naked and fighting him off. He did not like that and pulled out his favorite knife. The one with the serrated edge."

"Shit," he groaned.

"Yeah. He tried to get what he wanted first, shoving his hand between my legs and sliding his fingers into my body. I squirmed, kicking and screaming and that made him mad. He picked up the knife and started at my eye and carved slowly in a jagged path down to my mouth. It hurt. I called 911 but passed out before they got there and woke up in the hospital."

"Fuck. I'm sorry Jana. I'd like to fucking kill him right now."

That made me smile. "You hold him down while I do the honors?"

"You got it, babe."

"You're a good guy, Max. I hope you know that."

"I haven't done good things."

"You survived though. That's hard as hell, and it's the one thing people don't tell you. You know, I worried so much about the pain of my scar that it didn't occur to me to worry about how it looked until people looked at me like I belonged in a freak show. And no therapist, mental or physical, had prepared me for a lifetime of that."

"Ouch."

The beginning strains of *Rhiannon* began to play and I stood with a smile. This night was too heavy and when would I ever have a guy like Max all to myself for an evening? Never. "Let's dance. It's the perfect therapy!" I bounced and swayed, letting the music move me as I pulled him to his feet.

He laughed. "You're crazy."

"Maybe. But sometimes you just have to dance your ass off!" I held his hands, twisting and bouncing.

Twirling and doing a pretty bad job of finding a beat. But I laughed and then he laughed, both of us smiling under the moonlight and forgetting all about the shit life had heaped on us.

After three songs my jaw cracked in a yawn and Max stopped. "I should get home."

I could've asked him to stay, but I knew it wasn't a good idea. "Okay. Thanks for drinking and sharing your story with me."

"Anytime," he said in deep, sexy voice that made my nipples hard. I felt his gaze on my back as we walked through to the front. I turned at the door and he was much closer than I anticipated, giving me a chance to see the tiny flecks of green in his gray eyes.

"Thank you for tonight, Jana. I like spending time with you." His big rough hands cupped my face and slowly, his mouth found mine. His lips were soft but they moved sure and confident. His mouth felt like sunshine and heaven had a baby, making me feel warm and light and free. I gasped when his tongue touched my lips and he seized the moment, dipping into my tequila-flavored mouth.

My hands went around his neck, loving the heat emanating from his big body. I couldn't help, in my tipsy state, but notice our differences. He was hard as stone everywhere I was soft. Where I was warm, he was scorching hot. I let my hands roam the width of his back as he explored the depths of my mouth, making my body quiver with tension. It was more than desire. It was white-hot lust, emphasis on hot. I felt like I wanted to climb his body.

But he pulled back. "Damn." A satisfied grin lit up his face.

"Indeed."

He chuckled, pressed a short kiss to my lips and walked out.

Holy. Fucking. Hell.

KB Winters

Chapter 5

Max

"So that's the Cheese & Hearts platter with two types of wafers, the Six-ual Delights wine package with the Forty Days and Nights of Chocolates. Will that be all, sir?"

I sighed feeling like a goddamn fool, sending all that shit to Jana, but it seemed right. Hell, I wanted to. I hadn't stopped thinking about that kiss. For two damn days I could still feel her plump lips on mine, the taste of tequila on her mouth. On her tongue. I can't remember ever being lit so quick by just kissing a woman. It wasn't *just* kissing her though, the feel of soft, supple skin under my hands. She was such a fucking woman, so small and feminine that I wanted to sink into her and spend forever there. But I had to get to the clubhouse. "Yeah, that's all. Oh, wait, I want a card. *I had fun. Max.* That's it."

"Okay sir, thank you for your business. Have a good day."

"Yeah, you too." I stabbed the end button on my phone and grabbed my *kutte* and my keys. The Reckless Bastards clubhouse was actually a converted hangar at the ass end of Mayhem furthest away from Vegas. We liked the tourist action, because tourists spent big bucks on grass and ass, but they were too damn curious about the outlaw life so for the past two years we did our business on the border with the town of Henderson.

For the first time in too long, a smile touched my face as I entered the hangar we'd busted our asses cleaning out and converting and turning into multiple rooms. I walked in through the back at the long, black leather bar where one of the prospects uncapped a few beers. "Hey, Max!"

I waved at him and the Reckless Bitches perched on the bar, hoping today was the day they'd become someone's old lady. A few of the old timers sat at the tables drinking, watching the Bitches and prospects play pool and foosball. "Hey guys."

"Max! It's about fucking time." I turned at the sound of Savior's voice. He was the Sergeant-at-Arms for the club, and the craziest, happiest motherfucker I ever met.

"Savior, still rockin' that mountain man look, I see."

He scraped a hand over a full, chocolate beard and flashed a blinding smile. "The chicks love it, they think I'm a lumberjack and they can't wait to climb my log."

I laughed. "Crazy bastards. What's up?"

He shrugged. "I got some new guns and I thought maybe you wanted to play."

"Fuck yeah, I do." I fell into step beside him as we headed through what used to be the front door and out across the parking lot that still bore the signs for taxiing planes. A smaller building had been turned into a shooting range as a way to make use of all the land we got with the deal. And because we all fucking loved our guns.

"I got about a dozen different autos and semis because dudes love coming in here to shoot 'em, and they pay a fuck load of money for the privilege." Savior grinned back at me as we walked through the main retail area and back toward the stalls. "I got a good deal on 'em, too. Gonna get the prospects to review 'em later."

I laughed and shook my head because it was typical fucking Savior. "You really missed your calling as a cutthroat businessman."

"Nah. This way I get to make a ton of money without having the Man on my ass, and I don't have to fucking shave every day." He pulled out two pieces and we were quiet as we loaded them up and headed outside. "It's perfect weather for shootin'."

"Yeah." It was nice out and after sleeping a full night, I figured it was time to see how it felt being behind a piece of metal again. Squeezing the trigger to feel the quick jerky motions of an automatic weapon felt like coming home. Five seconds in and I already felt like I never stopped shooting, and I hadn't. Not really, but I had taken some time away from everything that reminded me of my past. This felt nice.

Until it didn't. I set the piece down, unloaded, disassembled and cleaned it while Savior kept firing with a shit-eating grin on his face. He whooped and hollered until he ran out of ammo, then he reloaded and started all over again. I watched him and the joy he seemed to have at something so simple and I envied that. "You want another weapon?"

I shook my head. "Nah, I'm happy to watch you shoot like a fool." And I was. Happy to watch him and let my thoughts wander to Jana. Eventually I stepped back inside when a few of the prospects came to test out the new hardware, the area got too loud and raucous.

"Looks who's returned to the land of the goddamn livin'!"

I smiled and looked up, way up and the biggest, baddest Army Ranger the world has ever seen. "Cross, what the fuck is up man?" I greeted our club president with a broad smile and a fist bump.

"Shit. Keeping the monkeys in line. You look good man, glad to see you around."

"Yeah," I sighed. "I'm trying something different, so we'll see how it goes." I didn't want to get into it, but I needed Cross to know I was working on my shit.

"Glad to hear it. There's some problem with the baked goods vendor and I need you to deal with it."

I nodded and headed to the office so I could take a look at what he was talking about. For the next few hours, I could admit that it felt damn good to get back into things, even if for just a little while. In the middle of arguing with the baker about their use of new ingredients, a text came in.

Thanks for the basket. Want to share it with me tonight? ~JC

I smiled. Big. "If you want to keep our business you need to make this right. I'll give you a couple days to figure out how." I hung up and sent a message back to Jana.

More than anything. Should I bring anything?

I held my breath and waited for her to respond. When she did, all the air sucked out of the room.

Just you. See you soon, Max.

Damn. And just like that I was hot and hard, and eager to see Jana. I moved like my ass was on fire, saving documents and writing notes for shit I needed to do tomorrow, or whenever I wasn't so distracted by a curvy blond with kind eyes. *Kind eyes?* That was how bad she fucked with my head and had me saying shit like *kind eyes*. What the fuck did that even mean? Dogs have kind, soulful eyes. Not women.

I needed to fuck her. I wanted to bury my cock deep, lose myself in a soft, willing female like Jana. No, not *like* Jana. I wanted Jana. There was something about her, maybe it was her sassy mouth or the way she seemed to just get shit that called to me. But I was too fucked up for more than a few nights of fucking, so what I needed was to satisfy my hunger, my lust and move on. Like always.

"Leaving already?"

I looked at Cross. "It's handled and something came up."

"I'll bet." He laughed as two Bitches lounged across his big body, wearing next to nothing but mile high stilettos. "See you around Max. Don't be a stranger."

"I won't. Later, brother." I headed back out into the sun, threw on my shades and helmet and aimed my bike toward my little house. I lived in a regular ass neighborhood and I did it on purpose. My CO, Brandt, had assured me that living among the people—the families and kids—I fought to protect would make shit easier. It did, but not in the way he meant. Kids didn't give a shit if you were grumpy, especially when their parents had them convinced you were a goddamn hero.

I wasn't a hero, but I couldn't tell them that, and the truth was I liked having those little faces look up at me like I was their God given protector. If I could bottle those looks and keep them for late at night when I couldn't sleep, I'd be fucking cured.

The block I lived on would be described by a realtor as *idyllic*. Trees lined streets wide enough for cars to park and pass with no problem. There were basketball hoops, goal posts, bases and bats littering the yards and sidewalks. Bikes were turned on their sides everywhere to serve as proof this street was run by the ankle biter set.

"Hey Mr. Ellison!"

The engine still purred when Elijah Walker called out to me. "What's up, kid?"

"How do you keep that motorcycle up?"

I turned and grinned. "The same way you stay up on your bicycle. Muscles and good balance."

"So if I can stay up on this, I can stay up on that?"

"Basically, but you need a lot more muscle and height before you can hold this baby up. You're too short."

He pouted but he considered my words. "Cool. Do you go fast?"

I looked over my shoulder at his house next door and found his grandmother smiling from the porch. I waved to her. "I love to go fast, but I shouldn't because it's dangerous."

"And you'll have to pay a ticket. My dad always swears a lot when he gets a ticket, says it's state-sponsored robbery."

I grinned. "Your dad is right."

His bright smile said he was happy with my answer as he slid back onto the seat of his bike. "Thanks Mr. Ellison. You think you can teach me to ride when I'm older?"

"Sure kid."

"See ya later, Captain!"

"Bye, Lieutenant!" He saluted for a moment before clutching the handlebars and letting his bike go as fast as his scrawny legs would allow. Yeah, living in this neighborhood had helped.

***

After a quick shower and shave, I got dressed and made my way to Jana's. With a gift. What the fuck was wrong with me? I never bought anything other than drinks or a meal for a woman I intended to take to bed. If they required any more than that, I moved on. The Reckless Bitches were always up for a hard fuck with nothing more than the hope of becoming something more. But here I was, buying a gift. Another gift.

Shit.

The door swung open and a woman who was not Jana answered. "Well, hello. You must be Max. I'm Teddy, the best friend."

I nodded as recognition dawned. I could see why Jana thought I might want her friend, she was beautiful with long legs, bright red hair and big blue eyes that offered just enough promise to drive a man insane. But she seemed high maintenance as fuck. "Nice to meet you. Yeah, I'm Max." I shifted the gift and shook her hand. "Jana home?"

She opened the door further and stepped back. "Yep. Don't worry, I'm not staying. I'm very happy to meet you Max but even though you look like you could snap me in half with two fingers, I have to tell you that I grew up in foster care and I know how to fight dirty. Don't hurt my friend."

Shit. "I have no plan to do that. I like Jana." I smiled. Like it would even matter.

She studied me, took me in as if she'd already measured me and knew my worth. Then her gaze shifted, maybe it softened, I don't know. It changed. "Good. Just don't let her stay in the house all the time. She's beautiful and she belongs out in the world."

"Just because I don't know what you're saying doesn't mean I can't hear you!" Jana's voice sounded affectionately annoyed from deeper in the house.

Teddy laughed and I removed my jacket and hung it up. "Don't worry, she's just threatening me." She laughed even harder and motioned for me to follow her. "Damn what smells so good?"

"You didn't think we were just going to eat chocolate and cheese, did you?"

I frowned at her question, scanning the kitchen to see she'd been up to some serious cooking. "I did, but I'm happy to be wrong. Can I help?"

"Damn," Teddy sighed. "You look like that and you're offering to help? Jana, you lucky bitch." She chuckled and wrapped her friend in a hug. "Have fun and be a little crazy. He's hot and he seems nice, and that's like a fucking unicorn."

Jana's skin flushed pink and she looked over her shoulder at me. "Your whispering game needs work, Teddy. Now get out of here."

She laughed. "I'm leaving. Be bad tonight. Very, very bad."

And then we were alone. "Sorry about that," Jana said with a sheepish smile. "She means well."

"She seems nice and she gives a damn, that's always a good thing in my book. But if you think I'd ever choose her over you, then I'll have to make sure you know that's not true before I leave tonight."

She sucked in a breath and released a shaky breath. "Put that smile away, please. Have a seat and tell me about your day. Booze or wine?"

"No beer?"

"Too filling. I like to drink and snack at the same time, and with beer you get too full to properly snack." She said it with the expertise of a neurosurgeon. "So?"

"Booze. I've never gotten into wine. It tastes okay, kind of bitter."

She smiled like that was the right answer. "Then I just have one question to see if this can ever be more than friendship."

I stared at her serious expression and wondered for a moment if I'd read her and this whole situation wrong. "I'm ready."

"Jack or Maker's Mark?"

In that moment, I thought I might've been half in love with her. "Maker's Mark of course."

She kept her face emotionless as she reached below the counter and pulled a bottle up. "This is the 46 but I think you'll like it."

"My mouth is already watering." A grin lit up her face as she poured two fingers into two hexagonally shaped glasses.

"Perfect. Let's toast to good friends, great booze and great kisses."

Fuck. "Hear, fucking, hear." Damn that hit the spot. "How'd you know?"

"I didn't. I work and live here, so I like to enjoy different things. Like cocktails. Bars aren't exactly my scene, but I like to drink."

Her face, that was why she didn't go out a lot. I could only imagine the assholes she came across, especially with the model beautiful Teddy at her side. "Nothing wrong with that." But I would try to do what Teddy suggested and take her out. Next time.

"So, your day?"

"It was good. Productive." I told her all about my trip to the club and getting back to it. "It felt weird because I've been, I don't know, vacant for so long. But everyone greeted me like I'd never left. It was weird."

"You loved it," she accused, lips pulling into a smile around her glass.

"I think I did. It felt like things were just back to normal. They weren't, but for a short period of time, I remembered who I used to be. It was nice."

"That's good. You look like you've been sleeping." A timer sounded and she turned, bent to look into the oven, giving me a great view of her ass cupped in blue denim. Heart shaped and more than a handful, I wanted to just fucking sink my teeth into it. "Damn," I groaned a little too loud.

I blinked and looked up into big, laughing brown eyes. "Sorry."

"Don't be. So, sleeping?"

"The night we kissed, I slept like a baby," I told her honestly.

She smiled and her pale skin turned bright pink. "Me too."

I let those words sink in, but more importantly their implication. "I couldn't think about anything but you all night, Jana."

"I know," she admitted and fanned her still reddening cheeks.

I couldn't help but laugh at how easily she blushed. "I can't say I've ever reacted to a kiss like that before."

"Like what," I asked, curious if she would answer. I knew I shouldn't push her—but then, I knew she could take it. I could tell.

"All hot and bothered," she answered honestly. Her skin still burned but she spoke plainly. "It was weird. Hot—but weird. I don't know." She shrugged and turned toward the fridge, sticking her head in the freezer for a few seconds. "Okay better. Ready to eat?"

I stared at her for a long time, letting my gaze rake over her until her skin pebbled with desire and her nipples peaked behind her t-shirt. "Oh, I can't wait to eat."

She sucked in a breath and I grinned. "You're bad."

"You have no idea." She really didn't, but I hoped this thing between us burned out before she had a chance to realize it. I liked the idea of being a good guy, a good memory for her.

"No," she said, tilting her head to the side and looked at me. "But I'm starting to think I might want to find out."

Chapter 6

Jana

"He'll be here soon, Teddy. Should I or shouldn't I?" I rolled my eyes even though she couldn't see me, the phone in a precarious position between my shoulder and ear while I pulled Francesco's from its delivery packages. I'd invited Max over for painting and more.

"I can't tell you what to do with your body, Jana. That's just wrong on so many levels."

Times like this made me wonder why I so desperately wanted friends. "Fine, do you think it's too soon to consider sleeping with him?" I knew after the first kiss that I wanted to lose my virginity to him, because no man had ever made me feel so wanted. So desired. And if I was going to open my body up to a man, it would definitely have to be one who made me feel like the most desired woman on the planet.

"No, I don't. He's hot and clearly he's hoping for a taste of you, I say go for it. Just go in with your eyes open."

I nodded as I put the risotto Milanese into a big ceramic bowl and covered it. Next was the chicken Marsala and then tiramisu. "Meaning don't fall for him?"

"Fall for him if you want, it might do you some good. But before you decide, ask yourself if you're okay with him walking away."

I froze. "You think he's going to walk away?"

"Honey no, but there's always that chance with men. Usually we don't know until it's too late. I think you should go for it, but if you let whatever happens between you and Max color what happens for the rest of your life, you'll regret it."

That didn't really give me any answers. Or hope. "Come on, Teddy, it's not like guys are pounding down my door and certainly not men like Max. I want, just once, to have sex with someone who wants me. Not just any warm body."

"Then there's your answer. Good luck and make sure you use condoms. Bye, love you," she said in one breath and hung up before I could ask another six dozen or so questions.

"Thanks Teddy," I grumbled and put the tiramisu in the fridge. Max would be here in the next fifteen minutes and I still needed to get dressed. We were painting tonight so I couldn't get too dressed up, but I opted for a lacy tank top to wear under my smock and a cute little denim skirt. It felt flirty and cute, like something a woman might wear on a first date. Or a third, if I didn't chicken out.

Okay, so maybe I kind of chickened out right away because when Max arrived, I already had on my painting smock. "I figured we could paint in the back until the sun sets. Then, we eat."

He grinned, a hungry look in his eyes. "I was hoping you'd say that." He walked beside me, our fingers lightly brushing as our hands swung back and forth. He smelled good, like what a man should smell like, outdoors and leather. Man and musk. I didn't know what exactly it was, only that it made me want to flare my nostrils just to take in more of his intoxicating scent.

"What are you going to paint tonight?" I didn't want to paint, I wanted to sketch and I wanted to sketch him.

He stopped dead in his tracks. "You mean you don't have a nude model or a plate of cheese for me?"

I laughed at his convincing delivery. "I would consider being your nude model but I'm afraid that the end result might give me body image issues."

He pouted and then his face transformed into a magnificent smile that made him look a decade younger. Lighter. Like a man without a care in the world, rather than a man with the weight of the world on his shoulders. "That's a good point and we can't have a body like yours thinking there's anything wrong with it."

The man was fucking potent and I had no protection against it. "Uhm, thank you."

"This is nice." He stopped and looked around the yard where the lights strung throughout my trees were on, providing a soft glow to the early evening sun. "What are we painting?"

"The setting sun."

He grinned again. "Suh-weet."

Quietly we both sat and began mixing paints and sliding our brushes across the canvas. I had bigger canvases than Moon had at her shop, but with the stunning view we had tonight, I didn't think it would be a problem. When I snuck a glance to my left, Max had already begun splashing red and orange paint across the canvas. His face was a rugged mask of concentration, so compelling that I knew I had to at least paint him now. I'd commit every plane of his face to memory to sketch later.

"Shouldn't you be watching the sky?" He grinned to show me he wasn't bothered at all by my blatant staring.

"Nah, you're a much better subject." I don't know what possessed me to act so bold, but his gray eyes flared with desire each time I did. I felt like I had some kind of power, but just power to turn him on. He wore an outfit that looked more at home on fifties biker gangs rather than what he was, which was so much more than a man who belonged to a motorcycle club. A crisp white tee clung to his massive chest and arms, looking even starker white against skin that had seen too many days out in the sun, and jeans. Good lord the man did things for jeans I didn't even think were possible. They hung low on his hips, hugged his thighs and ass and fell to a rumpled heap over a pair of well-worn leather motorcycle boots.

My whole body lit up like the Vegas night sky just looking at him, and that had never happened. Not even when I did research online. But I forced my mind to focus on the canvas and to look only at Max as a subject. At least until we were done.

Almost an hour later the sun had set and Max sat back. "I don't think mine is gettin' any better than this, sweetheart."

I leaned over and stared, stunned. "Max, this is really, really good." He'd captured the sky just as real and three-dimensional as it appeared. Hot and fiery, transforming the entire desert landscape around it. "Wow."

"Don't blow smoke, honey."

I laughed. "Not to worry. Really, it's great." He still didn't believe me, but that was okay. He would. If he stuck around, that is. "Dinner?"

He grinned and leaned towards me. "First let me see yours."

I put up a token protest just because I wanted to feel the heat of his body and when he stood behind me, staring over my shoulder at his own face, I got just what I wanted. "I know I should've asked but you were so deep in concentration and the lines ... well, I just had to. Be mad if you want, but I think it came out well."

"You're wrong. It came out fucking incredible." He leaned even closer and I knew what he was staring at, that small puckered scar just above his clavicle and before his shoulder. "You see a lot, Jana."

"From a lifetime of being an outsider. On the plus side, it has turned me into a pretty good judge of character. Let's eat."

He laughed behind me, but followed me in. We dropped the paintings in the formal dining area I never used because the kitchen had better light.

"Did you cook again?"

"Nope. I ordered from Francesco's. They have excellent food and I had too much to do to cook today."

"I would've taken you out to dinner," he said, his tone sounded upset and I didn't know why.

"I'm sure you would have, but I invited you over and it is customary for the person who extended the invitation to provide food, isn't it?" This moment and the uncertainty reminded me of the other reason I avoided relationships. There were all these emotional landmines you had to navigate, and the shit part was that you could do everything right and still get it wrong.

"Yes. I don't want you buying me dinner."

"Why? Is it because you're a man or because you think I don't have a lot of money?"

He sighed and grinned as he raked a hand through his hair. "I am the man and I should buy you dinner." He lifted a heaping spoonful of risotto into his mouth, chewing angrily.

I understood now. I remembered in college, the other girls all fretting about what would happen if they had to buy their own meals when they'd spent all the money their parents had sent them. I didn't have that luxury but I learned a lot about arbitrary relationship rules. "Fine, next time you come over, I expect to be fed. Happy?"

He grinned. "Sure, Jana."

We both dug in, absorbing the creamy carb deliciousness, at least I assumed so based on the relative silence. It wasn't an oppressive silence though and I didn't mind. It felt right. Like we didn't feel compelled to fill the void.

I was halfway through my second glass of wine, just enough to blur the edges but not enough to make me reckless. Or forgetful. "Max, I would like to have sex with you tonight."

He choked on the beer I'd bought for him. "What?"

"I would like to have sex with you tonight."

"Uhm, okay?" He stared at me like he was waiting for something, but I had no clue what. "I would like to have sex with you too."

My shoulders relaxed. "Oh, good. But what's so amusing?"

"Nothing, you're just very straightforward. I like it."

There was more, I could tell. Arms crossed I glared. "Tell me."

"I was just trying to figure out where would be the best place to start my seduction attempt."

"Really?" I had a feeling he was interested, but if he put this much thought into it, he must be as hungry as I am. He nodded. "You didn't know?"

"I wasn't sure. I-I'm not good at those kinds of things." But now that he'd mentioned it, I knew where we could start. "The sofa seems like a good place to start," I offered up.

He stood quickly, grabbing my hand and pulling me to the living room where he sat down and patted his lap. "Hop on."

I stared at him, mouth open in a way I was sure couldn't be less attractive as I shook my head.

Max laughed. "You'll end up here anyhow, let's just start there." He said it so easily, so reasonably, I couldn't possibly refuse. Could I?

Hell no. I slid, knees first, onto his lap, gasping right away as the zipper covered steel rod between his legs nestled right between my own thighs. It was long and hard, too long and hard considering a pair of silky panties were all that separated us. "Max," I whispered.

"Yeah, this was the perfect place to start," he said, smiling as one hand slid through hair I'd let air dry so it held sexy beach waves. The other hand slid up my thigh as he brought my head lower until our lips touched and then it was an exquisite inferno raging between us. It was so hot I could feel the smoke filling my lungs, feel the flames licking at my overheated skin as my body began to move in ways I didn't think possible. His thumb grazed over my pussy and I cried out.

"Oh! Wow!" It was spectacular and it never felt that way when I did it. "Max," I moaned as he slipped inside my panties, his warm hand, the rough pad of his finger gently rubbing at first, but his speed and intensity increased until it was a dance I seemed to know all the moves to as my hips rolled and I attacked his mouth the same way he attacked my body. With a single-minded focus. Pleasure.

"Fuck, you're so wet Jana." He tore his mouth from mine, hand still caught in my waves as he held me firmly, gray eyes staring deep into mine.

"I think you might have a little something to do with that," I told him and licked up the column of his neck. He was so hard and strong, muscular everywhere and I wanted to explore.

My hands went to his chest, grazing over sculpted pecs and down rock-hard abs until I reached his waistband. Then I reversed the journey, sliding under that delectable white t-shirt so I could really feel his body. "You're so big. So hard. I can't believe this is a real body." I sounded like a moron, but he felt surreal.

"Honey it's all real, and it's all yours."

"Take off the shirt," I ordered in a voice more commanding than I'd ever used in my whole life.

He grinned and did as I requested. "Happy?"

"Hell yes I'm happy. Max you're magnificent!" I leaned forward and slicked my tongue over the corded muscles between his neck and shoulder, lower to his pecs and the hard brown nipples that beaded under my efforts. The more he touched me, the more I wanted to touch and taste him. Every inch of him. "Oh, shit!" He sank a thick finger inside me and a low moan escaped.

"Fuck you are so responsive."

"Is that bad?" I asked and nibbled his ear as he continued to finger me, hard and deep and fast.

"Fuck no, it's not bad. No, it's a goddamn turn on. If my cock gets any harder, I'll probably hurt you."

That shouldn't have given me shivers, but it did. Sorry if I was betraying my feminist sisters, but I wanted him to fuck me until it hurt. "Okay," I panted.

"Say it again," he commanded, his voice dark and demanding. Confident.

"Okay," I said, moaning when a second finger joined the first, stretching me deliciously. It felt a little awkward but I was so horny, so aroused that I couldn't worry about that.

"Oh, Max! Max!" Two fingers were buried deep while his thumb flicked over my clitoris and I couldn't hang on a moment longer. I held his shoulders to keep me from floating away, because I was pretty sure it was about to happen...any moment now. My hips moved faster and faster, in time with his hand.

"Fuck my hand, Jana. I want you to come all over me. Now," he urged and nipped at my breast, sending me into an orgasm unlike any that had ever spilled out of my body. I was sure some of it had to do with the fact that someone else was giving it to me, but there was something about this man that just knew how to work my body.

"Oh. My. God. That was..." a shiver stole out of me and a satisfied smile crossed his face.

"It was hot as fuck is what it was," he said, calm but with an edge as he pulled his fingers from my body. "But now, I need something else," he said in a low, sexy voice and licked the fingers that had recently been deep inside me.

"Holy hell."

He grinned and smacked my ass. "You ain't seen nothin' yet, babe. Bedroom?"

I pointed down the hall.

***

My chest heaved and my breath caught in my throat as I lay on the bed in nothing but the pale blue lingerie I'd put on a few hours ago. Max stood at the edge of the bed, a dark look on his face, his own chest heaving as his gaze raked over every inch of my overheated skin. "Fuck, girl you're gorgeous."

I suppressed the urge to roll my eyes at his hyperbole and simply smiled. I knew what I looked like and it was enough that he wanted me. "I believe that's my line, Max. You are…incredible."

He flashed a dark smile filled with raw, hungry need. His hand circled my ankle and lifted my leg. His gaze never left mine as his hand slid up my leg to cup my calf all the way up to my thigh, gentle squeezes that felt like a massage if the massage was being given by the god of sex.

His hands slid up and down my legs until my whole body felt like the epicenter of a burning log, hot enough to singe but there were no flames in sight. He inhaled deeply. "I can already smell how much you want me," he groaned and just like that my legs began to come together. "Ah, ah, ah. Don't hide from me. I love that I can smell your desire."

My skin flamed with his outrageous words. As much as I knew about the act of sex, there were plenty of specifics I hadn't considered. Such as the smell of desire. "W-W-What does it smell like?"

He grinned. "Like sex and woman. Desire." His words left me too hypnotized to worry as he tugged my panties down my legs. "Like you want me as much as I want you."

Oh. "Well, I do."

He grinned that boyish grin that made my body and my heart do weird things I chose to ignore as his lips touched down on my ankles, behind my knees. The bones at either side of my hips. "Good. That's very good, Jana." His lips left a trail of white-hot flames climbing my body.

"Kiss me," he demanded and I did all I could when a man as big and masculine and commanding as Max issued a command.

I obeyed. I kissed him like his lips and tongue were the only things keeping me alive. I kissed him with a passion I didn't know I possessed, cupping his face and devouring his beer and saffron-scented mouth.

"You're an excellent kisser," I told him like I had any authority on the topic.

A lazy grin flashed. "You're not too bad yourself." Kisses rained down on me, my neck and shoulders. Grazing my collarbone gently before his mouth settled on the area of my breasts around the nipple without ever giving me the relief I truly sought. My back arched into his mouth and one hand cupped his head to keep him right there, to urge him to move a fraction of an inch where I needed him.

"Max," I moaned and finally, blessedly, his lips wrapped around that puckered nub and pulled so deliciously I felt the tug between my legs. "Oh, yes!" Back and forth he went, the delicious pressure on my breasts better, more sensitive, than I could have imagined. It was as though an invisible string connected my breasts and my pussy, pleasure for one caused pleasure for the other.

"Yes, Jana. Tell me what you want." His voice was harsh, low and gravelly as he kissed between my breasts and down my belly, his breath fanning the neatly trimmed hair above my pussy.

"You, Max. I want…you!" My hips bucked off the bed when his tongue swiped through the moisture of my core. "Wow!" That felt incredible and weird and I didn't know whether I wanted to move closer to him or farther away. He did it again and again and my feet began to tingle and I began to feel uncomfortable. "Wait, Max. Please."

He froze and looked up at me, eyes dark with desire and his hands gripping my thighs possessively. "Something wrong?"

Hell yes. "No, it's just you don't...have to do that." Teddy said guys didn't like it and I didn't want him to feel like he had to, especially when I felt so close to bursting.

"I don't have to taste you? What if I want to?"

He couldn't, could he? I didn't believe it but I didn't want to screw this up. I took a deep breath and opened my eyes to his. "I've never done any of this before. Not this," I motioned to his mouth hovering just inches from my most intimate area. "Not sex either. Any of it. But I want to, Max, with you."

He stared at me for a long time and I began to squirm, feeling like a science experiment gone wrong. Just as I had, hell even before the scar. The truth is that the scar had only made me feel like more of an outsider, already deemed an *other* because my parents had died. "How can that be?"

I fell back on the bed and covered my face. "Max, I like you. Enough to sleep with you when I haven't slept with anyone else ever. Please don't pretend with me. Not now. I couldn't take it."

"Wow. Jana, look at me." When I didn't, I felt the weight of his body over mine and his warm hands pulling my arm away from my face. "You're beautiful and yeah you have a scar on the right side of your face, but it's a small portion of a pretty great fucking face, okay?" I nodded at his serious tone. "And this body is the shit boys and men dream about, having a woman like this laid out before them so wet and needy," he said as a finger trailed down the length of my body, only stopping when it was knuckle deep inside me. "So ready."

When he said it like that, how could I resist. "Show me."

With a naughty grin, he kissed me. Long and hard and so intense I felt my body flood with pleasure around his finger, and only when he was satisfied that I was a complete pile of neediness did he kiss his way slowly down my body before settling between my legs. "Just relax. And feel."

I could do that. At least I thought I could; it was too much when he closed his mouth around my clit, kissing and licking, French kissing me down there, my body began to short circuit. No coherent thoughts formed in my mind other than '*Yes!*' and '*Max.*' His tongue moved like there were three of them, flicking my clit until it was swollen and aching, sliding deep into me, fucking me with his tongue until my legs clamped tight around his head. "Sorry," I panted.

"I'm not," he groaned and held my thighs open indecently. I propped myself up on my elbows so I could watch the sensual onslaught that had every muscle in my body trembling with an unnamed need. His lips closed on my pussy and he nibbled and sucked until my body fell back on the bed and went rigid for an eternity before long, body quaking convulsions rocked through me.

I don't know how long the orgasm lasted or how long his mouth remained fused to my body, but I knew I never wanted it to end. Ever. "Wow. So much better with a partner."

He grinned. "Oh you ain't seen nothin' yet." The words sounded like a promise to me and when he sat up on his knees, fingers grazing over sensitized flesh that made me shiver, he looked like some otherworldly warrior claiming a maiden after war. "It's going to hurt, Jana. I wish I could make it not true, but it will. But I'm going to do my damnedest to make it hurt as little as possible."

"I believe you," I whispered. It was true. I did believe him because he hadn't lied to me. Yet.

I watched, fascinated as he took the condom I placed on the nightstand and tore it open with his teeth, but watching him slide it over his long, thick—and face it, impressive—length was an erotic delight all on its own. He hissed out a breath when I reached out to touch him. "Not yet. I'm too close to the edge already."

"Good," I grinned.

"Damn good, but you're a virgin and your pussy is already going to test the limits of my control, sweetheart." To prove his point, Max lined up our bodies and pressed forward until just the head of his shaft was inside me. "Fuck."

I held my breath at the invasion. "It's okay," I assured him and at first it was. But as he sank in excruciatingly slow, inch by inch, I began to feel discomfort. A fullness I didn't know what to do with, a stretching that was both pleasurable and somewhat painful.

"It's not, but it will be." He pressed kisses across my chest and breasts, short, wet kisses that distracted me as he made short, shallow thrusts into me, using my moisture to ease the path. "Fuck, you're so tight," he groaned, flexing his hips until he surpassed that barrier that ended my virginity once and for all.

I sucked in a painful breath as he pushed through it and he froze. "No, don't stop. Please."

Warm eyes looked into mine and he pressed a quick kiss to my lips. "Your body needs to adjust. Relax."

Like I could fucking relax right now. But as I prepared a smartass remark, I felt my body relax around him and that's when it really started to feel not just good, but overpowering. "Ohhh, fuck," I hissed when I pulsed around him. "Okay, please Max."

"Say it again," he demanded.

"Please, Max. Show me."

Those must've been the magic words because he sank all the way in until I felt his sac smacking against my body, but the jerking motion pulled out slowly, leaving me cool and wanting before he thrust fast and deep. Fast and deep was his default, hips pumping furiously while my body scrambled to keep up. Eventually my hips found the rhythm and he grinned down at me. "You're good, baby. And fucking beautiful," he told me, grabbing my breasts with his full palms and squeezing as he pounded into my body.

I didn't think it would be like this, so intense, so *overwhelming*. The more pleasure his body brought, the more out of control I felt. My body moved, unsure if it was moving to him or away, only knowing that it needed to keep moving. "Oh, Max. I feel…" I didn't know how I felt. I just knew that I felt things. Maybe everything.

"I got you, babe," he promised and leaned down until his mouth touched mine. His kiss was slow and sensual, a sharp contrast to the raw intensity of the way his body moved inside mine. It was a contrast that my body responded to and when his tongue swept inside my mouth and his cock hit *that spot*, I exploded. My body shook so hard I was pretty sure I was having an out of body experience, watching our bodies twist and move erotically as one.

My back arched and a low, keening moan escaped as he continued to pound into me, grasping my hips hard enough to bruise as his hips kept up a punishing pace that wouldn't allow my orgasm to subside. It just kept coming.

And those strong, golden hips didn't stop moving until they surged deep inside, spilling into me as his orgasm shot out of him, making him buck and shiver with my name on his lips. "Jana, fuck." He collapsed on top of me, the weight of his body pressing into me.

I liked his big body on mine, his cock still pulsing and twitching inside me. His lips brushing light kisses over my sweaty sensitized skin. "Max, that was amazing. Thank you."

"That's my line, Jana. Believe me, the pleasure was all mine."

I laughed, feeling suddenly self-conscious at the way we were still joined. "I don't know, I think some of the pleasure was mine."

He grinned and pushed his hips so he slid deeper into my body. "If you only think, that means I need to show you again. Make sure you know for certain."

Oh. Shit. How did I, Jana Carter, land the world's sexiest man as my bedmate? I didn't know, but I learned long ago not question any moment of happiness that came my way and right now, I was positively fucking blissed out.

Chapter 7

Max

I should've already left her bed to go to my own, but I couldn't. First it was because she'd dozed off pretty quickly against me and I wasn't ready to let go of all that womanly flesh smashed against my body. But then her hand started a slow, hypnotic caress on my stomach that lead to a second round of fucking. Then we'd both collapsed in exhaustion and bone deep satisfaction and I'd been about to screw up my courage to leave while she slept with her back to me. But I looked over at miles of bare creamy flesh and my cock said we were staying.

But now Jana was out for the count and I was feeling damned uncomfortable. She'd been a fucking virgin hours ago, untouched by any man and like a fucking animal, I'd taken her again and again, with no regard for her own comfort. Not that she complained, but she was pumped full of fucking endorphins and that oxy-shit that made everything feel like unicorn dust. I should've said no. Just like I should be putting on my clothes and going the fuck home. I couldn't sleep here with her, not when I couldn't be sure how I might wake up.

The dreams still came every night. Some nights I could get back to sleep and some I remained sleepless, but the time I'd woken up and pointed a gun at one of the Bitches I'd taken to bed, I knew I couldn't risk hurting someone else. So I never stayed the night.

Until tonight.

I was a greedy bastard when it came to Jana, taking her over and over again, and even now I wasn't fucking sorry. Being inside her was ten fucking types of heaven and I couldn't get enough. She was exciting and hot, eager to please and so damn responsive it was all I could do not to push her limits just to see her respond.

Somewhere in between thinking of Jana's soft curves and going home, I must have dozed off because I was back in that fucking desert. Only this time the truck had already been hit and I was on the ground, trying to orient myself through the fucking smoke and flames. Shots fired in the distance and I looked to my left and my right, seeing a few of my fellow SEALs laid out, bleeding and shouting in pain but still firing their goddamn weapons. Finger on the trigger, I aimed through the smoke and squeezed that motherfucker, spraying the area.

It was too chaotic and my ears still rang and I couldn't see more than a few feet in front of me, but still I kept shooting until I heard that fucking click. Out of ammo. Scrambling on my hands and knees, my ass and elbows, I crawled to part of a body, Garcia, and grabbed both of his weapons and kept firing.

"It's okay Max, shhhh."

I blinked and looked around the desert to see who that sweet, soothing voice belonged to. But I couldn't see shit except a pair of black sandaled feet coming my way and I kept shooting.

"Max! Max it's all right. You're okay."

The images in the desert slowly faded and the voice became clearer. Louder. Jana. My eyes popped wide open and landed on the ceiling, but there was a warm, soft woman pressed into my side and a delicate hand caressing my head.

"You're dreaming," she whispered softly, oblivious to the way her tits pressed against my shoulder.

I froze and looked over at her before I sat up. Fast. "What the fuck do you think you're doing?"

She winced like I smacked her, using her arms to back away to the other side of the bed. Like she was scared of me. "You were having a bad dream or a flashback or something, I was trying to pull you from it gently."

"Well I don't need a fucking mother, Jana." The words spat out of me like venom and her big brown eyes were shocked at first, but that quickly turned to hurt and anger.

She gasped at my tone but quickly schooled her expression. "Right. Sorry." Slowly she set her feet on the floor and stood, walking silently to the bathroom and locking the door behind her.

Fuck! I was such an asshole. I sat there on the corner of the bed and stared at the wood grain and the deep green area rug under the bed. I shouldn't have lashed out at her the way I did, but dammit she shouldn't have tried to help. She should've worried about her own safety.

I sat there for I didn't know how long, but she finally walked out of the bathroom wearing a big thick robe that made her look smaller. More vulnerable. Her blond hair was pulled up into a messy bun on top of her head, leaving her scar looking red and harsh and angry. On full display.

I knew what she was doing, and I should have let her. But I didn't. I reached out for her but she stepped away from my touch. "Thank you for last night, Max. It was perfect." Her mouth smiled but her eyes looked exhausted and filled with anguish.

"I'm sorry, Jana."

She shook her head at me, her smile much too bright as she fought to hold on to the tears I saw welling in her eyes. "Don't be. I knew what this was. And what it wasn't." She turned and walked out the door before I could say anything, so I followed her lead.

I got dressed quickly and left without saying goodbye.

It was the least I could do for her.

***

"What the hell do you mean, 'It isn't that bad'? Weren't you listening?" I'd called Dr. Singh early Monday morning to see about switching my appointment this week because I spent the rest of the weekend alternating between guilt and drunken rage over how things went down with Jana. He could fit me in on Tuesday, one damn day early.

"I was listening but maybe you are in no position to see things the way I do." I appreciated his attempts at diplomacy, but I wasn't in the mood to be nice.

"Yes, you still had the dream, but she pulled you out before things got bad." He glanced down at his notes and I knew what he would say. "You said you don't remember anything after the pair of booted feet and you usually wake up with an elevated heart and blood pressure rate, cold sweats and panic attacks, right?"

I nodded.

"That *is* progress. And she is right, pulling you from that memory gently is less traumatic for the dreamer." He gave me a pointed look that only amplified my guilt. "Your friend is very smart."

"Who made her a fucking expert, anyway?" I knew I was well into bratty fucking kid status, but I didn't give a damn.

Dr. Singh nodded and crossed his legs, setting aside his ever-present notepad. "Military service members are not the only ones susceptible to post traumatic stress, Max."

I sat back and sighed, raking both hands through my hair. "Shit, Doc. I thought I wouldn't be able to feel any fucking worse. I was wrong." Naturally she knew what worked; she'd been dealing with her own trauma since she was sixteen years old. "God, I am such an asshole."

The good doctor looked amused. "Being an asshole can be fixed easily Max. It is called romance. What I'd like to discuss for the remainder of our time today is why you reacted the way you did."

"Shit, Doc, I already told you. I can't risk hurting someone because of my fucking dreams. My brain. That is not okay."

"But you didn't hurt her. Not physically anyway."

"Thanks for that."

"Avoiding an outcome isn't dealing with the issue Max. Maybe it's a good thing that you have a new lady friend right when you need one." A soft chime sounded, and I shot up out of my seat like it was on fire.

Dr. Singh stood slower and extended a hand to me. "See you next week Max. Sooner if you need me."

"Yeah, sure. Thanks."

"Remember, romance," he said to my back as I walked out of his office and the damn building like the fucking terrorists were after me.

The sun shone bright even through the overcast day but the chill in the air was typical of spring. I didn't really give a shit about the weather but that session with Singh hadn't helped. It made me feel guiltier, like the worst kind of asshole's asshole.

And worse, I probably behaved the way every man in Jana's life had.

I was so fucking tired of my own thoughts, I pushed the engine on my bike on the ten minute drive back to Mayhem, so lost in my own thoughts that I didn't see Savior until I damn near ran right into him. "What are you doing here?"

"Do I need a reason to come see you?"

"Cut the shit, Savior. What's up?"

Not that we weren't friends, we were. Savior was the only guy I really hung out with in the club because I didn't come to Vegas looking for a connection. I came in search of my brother and found two dozen others instead.

"Fine, I need you to make a run with me to Santa Fe."

"What the hell is in Santa Fe?"

"Guns. More to the point, we're delivering a couple crates to a gun shop who made the purchase through a show."

I blinked as the words seeped in. "I thought we didn't fuck with guns."

"We don't. At least not illegal ones. These are more on the legal side of the gray area and more important, we're charging a shit ton of cash for them."

I shrugged because it didn't matter to me as much as it should. Savior said they weren't breaking the law and I believed him. "Fine. When do we leave?"

"Today. As soon as you pack a bag. You heard from Golden Boy lately? Cross said he stopped taking calls."

"My calls and visits too," I grumbled. The only topic I wanted to discuss less than Jana was Tate. "I don't know what's going on with him but as long as he's not talking to me, I can't do shit about it."

"Call his lawyer, find out what's going on."

"Yeah, we'll see." I didn't have the energy to deal with anything right now. I just wanted to sit in front of my big ass flat screen and drink until I passed out. But it looked like I would spend the next twelve hours on the road.

At least I'd be too focused on the trip to think about the curvy blond who wouldn't let me have one thought that didn't include her.

Chapter 8

Jana

"I'm not upset with him, Teddy. I'm more upset with myself." I stabbed at the shrimp scampi I'd made and was no longer in the mood to eat.

She dropped her fork and flicked long red tendrils behind her before she rested her elbows on the table. "Bullshit. You should be upset with him; he was an asshole! You tried to help him and he bit your head off. That's on him."

I agreed, mostly. "But I shouldn't have been so hurt by it. That was an amateur mistake on my part when I knew what it was. I was too relaxed and I let myself forget what it was. Which was just one night."

"One night, my ass. At the risk of sounding like a cracked CD, that's bullshit. Your feelings are valid, dammit. Maybe you weren't expecting hearts and flowers and rainbows, but you were expecting common fucking decency!"

I let out a long, surprised breath. "Okay. You're right. I did expect him to act like a human at least until I locked the door behind him. But that didn't happen, so none of that matters." I had almost a full week to get used to it and yes, it did still hurt. But I would survive. Dwelling on it now wouldn't change the past, which meant it needed to stay buried.

"That doesn't mean you can't feel anything about it."

"I know and I have. But you know what, Teddy? I got up yesterday and looked myself in the mirror and reminded myself that as much this hurt right now, I've been through and survived worse."

"Well, shit. What can I say in response to that?"

"Nothing. I'm done talking about it. Tell me about your celebrity wedding." It was a jerk move when she was only trying to help but I didn't need to keep rehashing the best night of my life followed by one of the most humiliating mornings. I was there. I still felt it. Talking about it wouldn't change anything, but listening to her talk about work would be less stressful for both of us than watching her stress out about my feelings.

"Ugh, I don't want to talk about it. It takes place next weekend and then I can wash my hands of that woman forever. Makes me wish I'd charged more."

"Have you considered offering packages? Say one of those high rollers decides to marry his good luck charm but they want it done right. For let's say fifteen grand you'll whip it up in twelve hours, complete with mini bites and champagne." I was desperate, so sue me.

"Maybe. I have too much business right now to consider anything else. How about you? How's work?"

"It's work. Steady as ever. I'm picking up a new client, a green collective." I didn't care what it was, they were new business owners and their books were atrocious, which meant a lot of long hours creating and staring at spreadsheets. It was just what I needed right now. "Want to come to class with me tonight?"

"Afraid you'll run into Hot Rod?"

"No. Okay, yes. Maybe a little."

"No, I have a party to attend. I got an invite to this MTV party filming in that new nightclub in the Wynn, so I'm going to network. Or whatever." She rolled her eyes and stood, taking her plate to the sink. "Thanks for feeding me though, babe. You always have the best food. I think you missed your calling in the kitchen."

"I wanted to be a chef, actually."

She froze in the middle of the kitchen and turned to me, looking more shocked than I'd ever seen the unflappable Theodora Quinton. "Really? How did I not know this?"

"Because I don't talk about it. Ever. I cooked for an executive chef in Chicago because he was Michelin rated and I hadn't yet realized what a hindrance my scar would be. I was already there for school so that was also a factor. Anyway, I cooked and he loved it, then offered me a job as a dishwasher. I took it, thinking I had to work my way up like everyone else. Then one day he told me the truth. I was a talented chef and I could go far, but not if I scared the customers."

"That motherfucker!"

"Thanks. That was my sentiment too, at first. But Franco didn't say anything that wasn't true and I knew that, but I was young. I cooked a great meal and went out to get my praise. They were polite but they were horrified. Disgusted and uncomfortable. I thanked him for his honesty, finished my shift and changed my major to accounting. No one gives a shit what you look like if you keep their finances in order."

"I swear Jana, I just want to firebomb the assholes in your past."

I had to smile at Teddy's vehemence. "Thanks, but it wouldn't do any good."

"Well fuck them anyway, you're incredible." She got moving then, leaving her dishes in the sink before she wrapped me in a hug and breezed out the door, always in a rush.

I cleaned up and changed, leaving with just enough time to make it to the art store before class began.

"Hello, Jana. I wondered if you'd come tonight."

I grinned evenly at Moon. "This week was busy and I really needed to paint," I told her and she gave me a commiserating smile. My usual spot was open so I quickly took it and began to set up the supplies how I liked them.

"Jana, I'd like to speak with you a moment," Moon said nervously, wringing her hands on the crushed velvet dress that fell to the floor.

"Sure, Moon. What's up?"

"I'm doing a showcase of amateur artists and I would love to feature some of your oils and sketches. You have a good eye."

I sighed, a war brewing within me. I would love to show off my art, but just like chefs, people always wanted to meet the artist. "I would love to help you out Moon, but I can't." At her confused look I explained, and she looked horrified.

"No, that can't be. You're beautiful. That old thing is hardly noticeable, no matter how much you think otherwise." She waved her hand like it was inconsequential. A jagged six-and-a-half-inch scar was inconsequential. "Just think about it. Please."

"Sure, Moon. I'll think about it."

"Oh good." With the same, kind smile that was her trademark, she glided away and got class underway. Tonight, there were two separate hen parties, one for a twenty-something and the other for a late in life love affair. The women chatted happily, giggling and drinking, oblivious to my own turmoil that had nothing to do with Max's absence.

No, tonight's subject was self-portraits. My absolute favorite.

It was Friday and I had a bottle of vodka chilling in the freezer and long-neglected Netflix account to look forward to when I got home. It would be the perfect end to a long, emotional week.

Next week had to be better.

***

The good thing about having my own business was that I could choose my weekend. It turns out that vodka and Netflix hadn't been a suitable enough distraction and I spent the rest of the night going over the books for my latest client. Mr. Cross had warned me that the books were in complete disarray and it turned out that two martinis had been the perfect fuel to organize everything into stacks. Once that had happened, the rest of the weekend had kind of snowballed into hours upon hours of updating eighteen months of their nonexistent recordkeeping.

I'd been hesitant to take them on as clients because of the gray area of legality, but helping small businesses get their books in order and helping them save money to achieve their dreams was a rush unlike any I'd ever known. I used to believe there were people out there who got pleasure out of helping other people, but years of foster care had cured me of that foolish notion. At least until I took on my first small business. Mr. and Mrs. Chen had created a funky Asian fusion restaurant, but they'd had a difficult time getting the right clientele in the door. I freed up some of their cash for marketing and now they had one of the most popular eateries in Chicago.

I had that feeling all weekend, which was probably why I worked straight through, only stopping for meals and sleep. I knew how pathetic it was that I used work to get out of living the rest of my life, but helping this company wouldn't hurt me. I felt a brief sense of euphoria at helping but then it was business as usual.

Unlike men, who tended to leave their mark when they left.

So, I decided when I woke up at seven on Tuesday morning, that I'd take the day off, which meant lounging around in my pajamas while I cooked up a southwest omelet topped with my delicious jalapeno pineapple salsa. And I plopped down on the sofa, put my feet up and watched the news as I ate. I was feeling proud of myself, not sparing a thought for Max all morning until the pretty brunette anchorwoman forced him to the forefront of my mind.

"In local news today, Tate Ellison, convicted six years ago of killing a man in cold blood, has been released. For months, a team of law students and their professor have been working to prove Ellison's innocence, which he'd always proclaimed."

I sat there, completely fucking stunned as she went on. Max's brother, because they had the same stunning gray eyes, had been exonerated. After a series of hearings that amounted to a new trial with the admission of new evidence, he'd been freed. The footage was live, a younger, blonder version of Max strolled out of a municipal building with a wide grin that radiated happiness. He was tall and broad shouldered like his brother, thickly muscled arms draped over an older man and younger woman dressed like lawyers. My hand automatically shot out to my phone, but I froze. I couldn't call Max. We weren't friends. We were less than friends.

But this was about his family. A brother who might like family while he readjusted to freedom. It might've been a piss poor justification, but it was also the right thing to do. I dialed and the he picked up on the second ring.

"Hello?" Max's voice was thick like he'd been asleep and then I heard a woman's laugh and my body crumbled into the sofa. "Hello?"

I squeezed my eyes shut with a quick reminder that this was real life and Max had always been too good to be true. Sucking in a deep breath helped, but not enough. "I don't know if you've heard or not, but I just saw on the news that your brother was exonerated and he's out of prison."

I delivered the information calmly and hung up quickly, biting the inside of my jaw to keep from crying.

I had no right to these tears. It was foolish to cry over what amounted to a one-night stand. I knew my emotions were tangled up because I'd never had sex before so I let a few tears fall and banished the rest. I'd done a good deed and that was behind me. I had a whole day to myself and I planned to enjoy it.

After a quick workout in the basement, I cleaned up a bit and showered, then made a shopping list. If I had a list, something to focus on as I pushed the cart up and down the aisles, I wouldn't have to focus on the other shoppers. I wouldn't see them look at me and recoil or their children point and stare, and I wouldn't have to pretend I didn't notice or that it didn't hurt. Besides, my list kept me organized. It guaranteed I had all the ingredients I needed and wouldn't have to make another trip too soon.

My first stop was a gourmet shop that required a trip into Vegas proper for the soft, fancy cheeses that I loved along with wines that the big stores didn't carry. The place was all dark wood and cool glass cases, filled with cheese and cured meats, jams and chutneys. The place was small and the man who owned the shop was always kind, so I kept coming back. I always spent too much money in there, but on the upside, it forced me to buy more fresh veggies to combat all that cheese. I wasn't overly concerned with my figure, but I knew I needed to be healthy because there was no one to take care of me.

The next stop required several deep, cleansing and fortifying breaths before I could even get out of my car. The supermarket was forty rows of everything consumable, which meant at any given time there were dozens of people milling about inside. But I wasn't a scared little girl anymore and I took another deep breath and stepped out into the sunny day. I grabbed a cart, pulled out my phone and scrolled to my list, then kept my head down while I filled my cart with everything I would need this week.

Other than dodging a few guys who thought they were interested, the trip had been a success. But there was a group of young guys standing right outside the automatic sliding doors, smoking cigarettes and laughing loudly. I peeped their leather vests and I knew they were bikers. Other than television and the little Max had told me, I didn't know much about them, but I knew men. They were trouble.

I put my head down and fingered my hair over my shoulders to shield my face, and pushed the cart through the doors, moving quickly through the clouds of cigarette smoke.

"Hey, baby!" They all laughed because this was apparently the best joke they had to offer.

"And look at that ass, so round and juicy," another called out but I didn't stop or turn, I pushed the cart with one hand and dug for my key ring with the other.

"I said, hey," a voice called but it was much closer to me and my heart picked up as my fight or flight instinct kicked in.

My left hand wrapped around the keychain and yanked it out just as a hand landed on my shoulder. I turned and pushed my right hand out and up, striking him in the throat.

"No!" My heart was racing too fast to process anything other than safety and I turned, pushing my cart at a jog to get to my car.

"Crazy fucking bitch!"

I grabbed both bags and shoved them in the back seat, not caring that both tipped over as I slammed the door.

"You're not worth the trouble, ugly bitch!"

I whirled around, keys in my hand with my fingers wrapped around the miniature bottle of pepper spray.

"I didn't ask for the trouble of your *unwanted* attention, asshole!" I yanked open my door. More footsteps fell behind me in quick succession, and voices began to shout. I blocked it all out and slid into my car.

A hand grabbed my arm and called out to me.

"Jana."

Max.

"Leave me alone," I shouted, staring up at him and wishing I hadn't looked up. "Please," I damn near cried as I started the engine.

"Jana," he said, my name an anguished cry on his lips, but I couldn't let myself be moved. As soon as his hand went slack on the door, I grabbed the handle, pulled it closed and raced out of the parking lot like a bat out of hell.

I raced home where I planned to stay for the next week. Or forever if I could find a place that delivered groceries.

Chapter 9

Max

"What the fuck is your problem?"

I wanted to wrap my hands around this fucking prospect's neck and squeeze. Not only had that motherfucker manhandled Jana, but he'd terrified and insulted her.

"Do you get off on touching women without their permission? That shit is for little boys. Are you a little boy?"

"Fuck no," he spat out but I saw the fear flash in his eyes. He knew I wasn't a man to be fucked with.

"She wasn't worth it anyway, ugly bitch."

This time I did pop him in his fucking mouth. "Like I thought, a little fucking boy. If you can't handle rejection maybe you should stick with the Bitches. And that 'ugly bitch' as you called her, is mine. Watch yourself, motherfucker."

My chest heaved, as angry fire swept through my veins. Seeing him touch her like that had unleashed something in me, something dark and angry.

"How the fuck should I know that?" he whined. Whined like the little fucking girl he was.

"That's the point, asshole. Don't go putting your hands on people without asking. Maybe we ought to hand you over to the Pink Ladies for a while," I laughed, referencing another club filled with men who didn't turn away sex based on gender. They rode and sold drugs, but they kept their business out of Mayhem, so we let them live.

"What the fuck is that supposed to mean," he said, getting up in my face like he wasn't just a prospect.

"It means, maybe if we let someone bigger than you touch you against your will, you might fucking understand what you did wrong." I was heated and ready to fight. It wasn't all on the prospect, but he was here and I didn't give a fuck.

"Max, man, chill the fuck out." Savior got in my face. "What the hell is going on?"

"What's going on is maybe we need to rethink who let into this club," I told him with a pointed look at the now fearful prospect. I gave Savior a quick recap of what had gone down. "That shit ain't right, man. Even if it wasn't Jana, you don't grab a woman who doesn't show interest. Or do we now?"

Savior's nostrils flared in anger at my intended dig at the Reckless Bastards. "He's a brother, we'll talk to him."

"He's not a brother yet, and she is the reason I've gotten any sleep over the past couple weeks." Jana was also the reason I hadn't slept it all this past week but that wasn't the point. "Look Savior, I get what you're saying man, I do. But what happens if she goes to the cops? What that fucker did was assault. That would be the perfect excuse for Sheriff Woodley to come toss the compound."

I could see the gears turning in Savior's head because he knew I was right. "Fine, I'll have Cross talk to him and make him understand how Reckless Bastards are expected to act."

That was as good as it would get, I suppose. "You guys got everything under control for the party?" As soon as I got the call from Jana this morning, I spread the word and the guys had begun preparing for a welcome home party for Tate. So far, I hadn't heard from him and that pissed me off, but all I could do was wait. And assume that eventually he would call me or come to the clubhouse.

Until then, I needed to see Jana. Talk to her. It might help if I started with an apology. Even as I started up my bike, I knew an apology wouldn't be enough. The way she looked at me, like I was no better than the asshole who manhandled her, had gutted me. I knew I hadn't handled things well, but I only felt like a piece of shit when she looked at me like I was one. She might not even open the door for me, but as I turned on her block I knew I had to find a way.

I walked slowly up her driveway and knocked on the door. While I waited for an answer, I scanned the neighborhood made up of all family homes but given the lack of bicycles and toys on the lawns and sidewalks, I figured this must be a block for young professionals. Jana would've done her best to stay away from inquisitive children with no filter.

The door opened and a wary expression crossed her brown eyes. "What the fuck do you want?" She didn't even open the door all the way.

"I was hoping we could talk."

She shook her head. "Well we can't. Please leave and don't come back." She pushed the door to close it and I slammed my palm against the door to keep it open. She gasped, brown eyes widened with fear. "What the hell?"

"Five minutes. Give me five minutes and then I'll go."

She relaxed her hold on the door. "I guess I shouldn't be surprised," she said and took a step back. She walked through the living room and into the kitchen, giving me a long look at her delectable heart-shaped ass and shapely toned legs in the softly swinging dress she wore.

"Speak." Jana stayed on the other side of the island counter, glaring at me like I might attack her at any moment.

"I was an asshole."

"No argument here."

I grinned but there was no amusement on her face. "I shouldn't have lashed out at you like that. It's just that—"

"Nope," she shook her head furiously and fisted her hands on her hips. "You were right. I am not your mother. In fact, we're not anything other than a memory. Don't worry yourself about it, Max."

"I know damn well you're not my mother, Jana. That doesn't mean I should've said that bullshit to you. And I am sorry, I was just worried and I'm not real good at showing those kinds of emotions." I felt like a fucking asshole sitting here talking about my feelings while she kept a whole damn island between us, but I needed her to know. "It wasn't about you. It was about me, and that's not a line."

She closed her eyes, trying to block the onslaught of words. "Fine Max, I accept your apology. Happy?"

"No. I've missed you."

She scoffed. "You're horny again, which is strange because you were with a woman when I called about your brother."

Dammit. I wasn't sure earlier if she'd heard Brenna or not, but she had. "I wasn't with any damn body," I shot back angrily. "You want the truth or you just want to believe the worst of me?"

To her credit, Jana took a moment to think about it. She was a logical, levelheaded woman so I knew she would take the question seriously. "I'm not sure, but I am curious so tell me."

Shit. "My club, the Reckless Bastards, we might not share a lot in common with some of the other motorcycle clubs but we're men. There are always women, a certain type of woman who wants nothing more than to be a biker's old lady. They are willing to do anything—*anything*—to become one, including sleeping with whoever is available in hopes of being promoted from a Reckless Bitch to an old lady."

She didn't say anything for a long time. "Wow." She turned to the fridge and pulled out two brown bottles, sliding one to the edge of the counter for me. "So it doesn't count?"

"It doesn't if I didn't fuck her. And I didn't. Brenna came in as soon as I picked up the phone, hoping to tempt me to fuck her. I wouldn't have fucked her anyway, but after your call I spent the next few hours trying to find my fucking brother."

Her demeanor changed instantly. "Did you find out anything?"

"Nope. He hasn't called at all. The guys are getting ready for a party, but now I don't even know if he'll fucking show."

Jana sighed and nodded as she walked around the counter, taking a seat across the table from me. "This isn't about you, Max. I know you don't want to hear that, but it's the truth. Your brother did six years of someone else's time and that's not an easy thing to come back from. He might not come around for a while." She shrugged. "Or he might be on his way to your club room right now. My guess is that he's decompressing with the people who helped free him."

"Shit, you're right. Thanks." I laid a hand on top of hers, grateful that she hadn't pulled away in disgust. "Still, he's cut me off completely."

That made her pull back for some reason. "You ever think it might be because of your club?" Her words held no venom, but they pissed me off all the same.

"What the fuck does that mean?"

She pushed back from the table and stood, abandoned her beer just to get away from me. "It means being associated with a biker gang might have hurt his chances to gain his freedom." She sounded exasperated, like I was the one being unreasonable.

"We are a club. A legal fucking club."

She shrugged. "Fine, I'm wrong. You should probably go check on the party." And right before my eyes, I watched her shut down. Pull away from me and shutter her emotions.

"Come with me."

"No." She crossed her arms over her body in a protective move that spoke volumes.

"Why not?"

She sighed. "Because Max, I may not be much to look at, but I am a real person and I deserve respect. I doubt I'll get that at a place where men treat women like you and your friends do. Have a good life, Max."

I stood and followed her back to the front door where she held a death grip on the doorknob. "You can be pissed off at me all you want, Jana. I fucking deserve it. But I like you and I'm not ready to say goodbye."

"Too bad it's not just up to you."

I grinned. "Maybe not, but I have my ways." She was ready to protest, to tell me what a fucking prick I was, but before she could take a breath my mouth was on hers, tasting and teasing her lips while she tried to resist me. The minute she gasped, I slid in and when our tongues touched, she tightened her hands on my arms, hanging on. A second later she was a full participant in the kiss, licking my tongue and nibbling my lips.

The kiss was hot as fuck, making my cock hard as she rubbed up against me. I lifted her in the air and her legs went around my waist so I was nestled right against the heat of her pussy. She moaned and my hips pressed harder, eager to be closer to where she was hot and wet, and so fucking tight for me. "Jana," I growled as my lips went to her neck, licking across her collarbone while she clung to me.

I wanted her more than I wanted to fucking breathe, but I knew I couldn't. Not with our last encounter still fresh in her mind. Despite her eagerness right now, I knew she wasn't up for fucking. But I needed to touch her. One thumb slipped into the elastic of her panties and found her clit, fat and swollen, her pussy already drenched with desire. "Fuck," she moaned and bit my ear.

"Jana," I groaned again and adjusted my hold on her because I needed to hear her soft cries of pleasure, her moans and gasps. It was torture as my cock hammered against my zipper, but all I wanted was to feel her come apart on my hand.

Her fingers dug into my skin and her hips moved, fucking my fingers as they plunged in and out of her. "Oh, god. Yes!"

Fuck, those eager sounds she made. Jana didn't hold back when it came to pleasure and she had no fucking clue how hot that was. I added another finger to her pussy, using my thumb to rub fast circles in her clit. "You're so fucking tight, babe."

She growled and tossed her head back. "Max."

"Let it go, honey. I've got you. Come all over me. Now."

Big brown eyes stared at me, full of wonder, as I plunged in and out of her pussy and then she fell apart, trembling around my fingers. Pupils dilated so her eyes were pure black, chest heaving as she rode out her orgasm. "Damn," she sighed. "Thanks."

She let her legs fall down until she slid down my body. "No baby, thank you," I told her and licked my fingers clean. "That isn't enough, but for today it'll have to do." She looked confused. Good. I was confused by it all too, but I was nowhere near ready to be done with Jana. I kissed her again, hot and hard, and intense as fuck. When I pulled back she was gasping, wide-eyed and shocked. "See you soon, Jana."

Chapter 10

Jana

"Are those extensions?" A woman with yellowish blond hair shouted across the room at yet another Friday night art class.

I glanced up and shook my head. "Nope, it's all mine."

"Damn," she pouted. "I was totally gonna ask who did them. Lucky bitch." She grinned and shook her head before returning to her friends.

Class hadn't yet started but the book club women had arrived about ten minutes ago and cracked open a bottle—or two—of wine, so things were rowdy already. I sat in my usual spot and kept to myself, sketching in a small pad until class began. The week had been long but productive and I really needed to blank my mind out for a couple hours, so I was happy when Moon stepped into the center of the half-circle and introduced the dancers we'd paint tonight. They were dressed in white and nude bodysuits, frozen in motion.

I pulled out my paints and began mixing when the bells above the door sounded, followed by the heavy *thud* of boots. Not just any boots. Motorcycle boots. I knew, before he even took the seat beside me, it was Max because my body told me. The tiny hairs all over my body stood up, electrified as my skin began to heat up. "Sorry I'm late," he called out to Moon. "Hey," he whispered to me, but I wasn't interested.

I kept my gaze fixed on the dancers, focusing first on the way they were connected from the collarbone to the hips. I focused on the shadows that would add depth to the overall image, gently filling in the other spots. It was harder than I thought, ignoring Max and his attempts at conversation, but I knew that I had to it. As good as his body had been to mine, the rest of it was too risky. I didn't take risks because I wasn't willing to pay for the consequences.

"There's too much shit here," he grumbled, struggling to focus his painting. "I know you hate me, but help me out. Please."

It was the passion in his plea that did it, forced me to speak to him. To look at him. "I don't hate you, Max." I didn't. I blamed myself more than him for how things played out. I knew better than to have expectations, but the sex was so good it made me forget. "Focus on one thing to start, like the way the legs are entangled."

"And then?"

I shrugged, trying to hold back a smile. "By the time you're satisfied with it, class will be over." He flashed a grin at me and I sucked in a breath at just how handsome he looked. I kind of missed out on the going crazy over boys part of life because I'd been in the hospital and foster care when I should've been kissing boys and going to school dances, so it made sense that a man as potent as Max could easily turn me inside out.

"Smart woman."

Not that smart, I thought but I kept it to myself because being snarky wouldn't change anything.

"That's me. Smart woman." I was smart, not beautiful. Being around Max was too hard and I refused to let my gaze wander anywhere other than from my canvas to the dancers and to the paint. I'd nearly relaxed when Moon dismissed us for the night.

"Jana, a word please?"

My shoulders sagged, but I was grateful to Moon for the temporary distraction even though I already knew what she wanted to talk about. The art show she was hosting and my role in it. I hadn't decided yet even though Teddy thinks it would be good for me, but I also had a feeling Max would try to talk to me and this way he might get tired of waiting.

"What's up, Moon?"

"Have you given any more thought to the show? I was thinking two sketches and two paintings." I was preparing my next excuse when she kept talking. "Just show up and see how you feel. If you're not up to mingling, tell me on the night and I'll say you're shy or something. Okay?" When she looked at me with those kind, pleading eyes that looked otherworldly with her long silver hair, I could only say one thing.

"Fine, Moon. I'll stop by later this week with some options for you."

Her face lit up with joy and excitement and I felt a small rush that my answer had pleased her. "Oh honey," she pulled me into an unexpected hug that felt natural and soft and warm. I couldn't remember the last time I was hugged like that. "Thank you so much. This will be fantastic, I promise."

I wasn't so sure, but these classes had given me contact with the rest of the world and in Moon, I'd found something like a friend. "If you say so."

"I do. Have a good night, dear." She waved me off with a knowing smile on her face that I ignored. I shouldn't have, I realized as I stepped outside and my gaze landed on Max, looking delectable as he leaned against the brick façade, one booted foot on the wall while he stared up at the sky.

"I wondered if you'd gone out the back to avoid me."

I laughed but the sound was bitter. "Yep, because it's all about you, Max."

His smile dimmed. "Okay, maybe not *all* about me. Grab dinner with me."

"Not hungry," I told him quickly. Too quickly because my stomach piped in to prove me a liar. "I'm going to eat when I get home," I quickly amended.

His lips spread into a slow, killer smile that made my entire body waver. I'd never seen a smile do that before and certainly I'd never experienced it. "Come on. I'm buying." He took my hand and I let him because I was too weak to resist. But a girl had to draw the line somewhere.

"I'm buying dinner."

"Let's argue about it later. What are you in the mood for?" He tugged me closer until I was practically nestled under his arm and he dropped a kiss on top of my head.

"There's a steak and seafood place just a few blocks that way." The place always did a steady business, but it was a higher end place and more importantly it was dimly lit. Max held me close the whole way, his hand still clutched mine as we walked through the restaurant toward our table.

He took the seat across from me and I took a moment to soak in his appearance. He'd be best described as ruggedly handsome but tonight his facial hair was overgrown, giving his sharp edges more depth and darkness. It enhanced his whole brooding thing. His gray eyes looked like melted down silver and his lips were lush and pink, making it hard to look away from that bottom lip that I'd learned was imminently bitable. And thoughts of biting Max immediately brought me right where I didn't want to be, smack dab in the middle of another fucking fantasy, or maybe it was a replay of the orgasm he'd given me last time I saw him.

His lips curled up. "I wonder what's on your mind, Jana." His tone indicated that he did, in fact, know.

I was quiet, but people often mistook that to mean I was shy. Those people were wrong and after a moment of thought, I decided to go for honesty. There was no reason not to be, since we were nothing but former lovers. "I was thinking about the orgasm you gave me up against the door."

He blinked, choked on the beer the waitress had set in front of him, and wine for me. "Good, because I haven't stopped thinking about it. Sometimes when I wake up in the morning, I can still taste you on my tongue."

I swallowed hard and squeezed my thighs together, grateful for the long white tablecloth. "You're too damn male, I swear," I told him and I heard the frustration in my voice.

Instead of being upset or offended, Max laughed. "I don't believe that's a thing, but I am glad to know I still affect you."

"I never said you didn't. But it's probably best we keep that night where it belongs."

"Right here between us?"

Damn him. My gaze narrowed and he laughed again. "No, right here," I told him and tapped the side of my head.

"Pity. Because all I can think about is doing it again."

A shiver shot through me involuntarily and I swallowed a humiliated groan. He just laughed, amused and filled with masculine pride at the whole situation. "Max. We can't."

His smile dimmed. "I know." The air between us changed, shifted from lighthearted and shallow to serious. "I owe you an apology, Jana. A real fucking apology. You have every right to be pissed off at me, but I need you to know that it's me, not you. As cliché as that sounds."

"It does, but I'm listening." I was also drinking, because I could only have this one glass of wine and right now I needed it more than the air traveling down my lungs.

His smile was grateful. "The dreams I have, sometimes they fuck me up. Bad. I appreciated the way you pulled me from that dream; it must have been fucking terrifying for you. But my reaction was, apparently, based on embarrassment."

"Understandable." I'd dealt with those same feelings in the years after my foster father attacked me, so I did understand. But I couldn't get over how cold and callous he'd been just moments after we made love. No, we had sex. Maybe we fucked, I wasn't sure but I would find out from Teddy later.

"So you forgive me?"

"Do you really need my forgiveness, Max?" I didn't get the feeling I was all that important to him, so my opinion should be irrelevant.

"I do. I like you Jana and I would hate it if you thought that careless bastard from that morning was me. It's not."

That much, I did believe. "Have you heard from your brother?" It was a clumsy change of topic, but I didn't really do emotion and certainly not in public.

His gray gaze narrowed but his lips curled up as if he knew what I was doing but didn't want to call me out. I shot him a grateful smile. "No. Not one fucking call or text to tell me that he was free or where the fuck he is."

I could see he was getting upset about it and I understood, but his anger wouldn't make Tate reach out any sooner. "The good thing is that he's out of prison, Max."

He gave me a strange look, one I couldn't decipher. "Sometimes I think you're too good to be true."

That was a first. I don't think anyone has ever thought that about me, much less ever said it aloud. I smiled as a warmth spread throughout my body. Our plates were empty as were our glasses, which meant dinner was over. Max would go home, hopefully alone, and I would definitely go back to my place and spend the night alone. Wishing I wasn't. "You think so?"

"I do."

"Thanks." I slid my bankcard into the leather booklet to pay the bill and grinned when his hands flexed with the desire to reach for it. "I appreciate you keeping your word about dinner."

"I wasn't going to," he grumbled.

"I know," I told him and licked my lips because my mouth ran dry at the sight of his smiling lips. "I never got a chance to just make out with a guy until we were breathless and hot and too out of our minds to make good decisions."

His big hands tightened on the tablecloth, nostrils flared as fire swept over his skin. But the waitress returned so I could sign the bill and he had to wait. The moment she was gone, he sat forward. "Is that an invitation?"

"No, it's a request. Can you fulfill that request, Max?"

He stood, practically knocking the chair over as he grabbed my hand and pulled me out of my chair and out of the restaurant. "Damn right I can."

I grinned to myself. I was asking for trouble, but making memories was better than having none.

At least tonight it was.

***

I woke up slowly, struggling to stretch with the big beefy arm draped over my waist. Max. He was hot and hard, like my own personal furnace. Not that I needed it, especially after that hour-long make out session on the sofa. My body had burned up, liquid heat coursing through my body as I straddled him, grinding against his cock while he kissed me silly.

No matter that I'd begged him to make love with me, to fuck me, he wouldn't. He said I had to be sure, so he carried me up the stairs, laid me out on the bed and spent hours exploring my body with his mouth and his tongue. He brought me several glorious orgasms that left me weak and sated, and when I turned to return the favor, he'd simply tucked me against his body and fell asleep.

I appreciated it because Max had made me feel not only sexy and desirable, but precious and cherished. Like I mattered.

And this morning I wanted to show him how much it meant to me. I turned in his arms because escape wasn't an option, his hand dropped to my hip as I took in the rugged cut of his jaw, the long dark lashes fanning his cheekbones. He had a masculine beauty that was hard to describe, but I'd spent more hours than I would ever admit sketching that face.

His chest rose and fell, dislodging the sheet as I adjusted to get a better look at him. His chest was so big, a deep grove ran between his pecs and down to his abs. My hand traversed the path, gaze riveted on his scarred, tan body. His cock twitched and began to come to life and I grinned. The moment was perfect.

Slowly I slid down his body, careful not to wake him so I wouldn't lose my nerve. I hadn't gotten a chance to really look at him last night or the night we made love. Had sex. He was gorgeous, his cock long and thick. Now that I held it in my hand, stroking gently, I pegged it as nine solid inches of hard—and getting harder—cock. I leaned forward with a tentative flick of my tongue across the slit on the head and the bead of liquid there. It was salty but also intoxicating.

I lowered my mouth to the thick mushroom head and wrapped my lips around it, pulling it into my mouth and allowing the length and weight of it settle on my tongue. It didn't have a taste, not really. It was slightly musky and smelled like Max, but the more I licked and sucked, the thicker his scent became and the wetter my thighs were.

"Ah, fuck," he bit out and my eyes flicked up to meet his, dark and intense. "Jana," he grunted, "you know how to welcome a man to a new day." He grinned but I could see the clench of his jaw, the way his nostrils flared.

I sat up, unable to read his body language or facial expressions. "Am I doing it wrong?"

"Honey, if you did it any more right, I might be fucking that dirty little mouth of yours."

I swallowed, his gaze and sensual tone went straight to my clit, making it swell. My pussy flooded with desire and I grinned. "That sounds intriguing. Will it hurt?"

"No, but Jana, you don't want that."

I shrugged. "How will I know? I want to make you crazy."

"Keep doing what you were doing," he assured me and with a proud smile, I bent back down and took him in my mouth, taking more of him in my mouth until the tip of his cock hit the back of my throat and he shouted my name. My pussy flooded again at the sound and I did it again, sticking a hand between my legs to see if it worked. Sure enough, my pussy clenched around two fingers when I took him deep. When his hips flexed and those sexy totally masculine sounds came from his mouth.

I did it again, this time trying to lick his balls as I did and his hips flexed again, so deep I choked, but it turned me on too. I should have been worried, at least, but all I could focus on what how this made both of us feel. The more I pushed him, the more his hips moved and he began to fuck my mouth like he said. I moaned and flicked my tongue against the underside of his balls.

"Jana," he warned in a deep, dark voice. I ignored him, too lost in pleasing him to understand his tone. His cock tightened on my tongue, hardened and then I felt the first trembles of his orgasm and then his cock shot hot spurts of liquid down my throat, salty and thick. Intriguing.

I slowed my mouth and only stopped when he pulled me away. "What?"

"Why didn't you stop?"

I frowned at his tone. "You didn't like it?"

"I didn't say that."

Okay, now I really was confused. "I felt how much sucking you off was turning me on and I wanted to see how far it could go."

"And," his lips curled into a sultry smile. "Come here." I climbed up the bed beside him and he slid two fingers deep inside me, pulling a satisfied moan from me. "Shit, babe. All of that from sucking my cock?"

"Apparently."

"Well honey, you can suck my cock anytime you need to get yourself in the mood." I laughed and smacked his chest but he grabbed both of my wrists and his expression sobered. I swallowed, suddenly wary.

"But now I feel compelled to return the favor."

I blinked. "It wasn't a favor." I didn't want him to do anything because of some tit for tat system of payback. "And you're not quite ready yet," I said, glancing down at his cock.

Max laughed. "That's okay, I have something else in mind." He slid down until his head rested on a pillow. "I want you to put your pussy right here," he said and stuck out his tongue.

I shook my head. "I can't."

"Oh you can. And you will." He pulled me until I straddled his chest. "Scoot up," he urged and though I moved tentatively, I did settle right over his mouth. "Perfect."

He palmed my ass until I leaned forward, hands braced on my headboard. Then his tongue, slightly cool to the touch, slid through my drenched lips, the sound so loud I cringed with embarrassment. "Oh, god!" My own hips began to move as his tongue and lips worked my body, flicking and sucking and bringing me so close to the edge, I could smell the freedom below. "Ah!" I couldn't stop moving, not when below me Max growled and licked like me and my pussy were his life force. "Max, oh fuck, Max!"

He gripped me tighter, holding me at his mercy while his lips pulled my clit and sucked it hard. Millions of shards of lights flashed behind my eyes, my body jerked and convulsed as the orgasm washed over me. I had a white-knuckle grip on the headboard, my hips grinding against him until he'd wrung every stitch of pleasure out of body, leaving me limp and boneless.

My body sagged against him and one long finger slid deep, sending me back up over that edge of pleasure one more time as he growled and kept sucking my clit until I was so filled with pleasure, my body was so slick with desire that my legs gave out. "Fuck, that was worth being nearly suffocated to death."

I laughed and rolled off him, resting my head on his chest. "That was like a drug. I felt naughty and kind of dirty." I kissed his nipple and he groaned. "I liked it."

"Good, I'm glad. Now let's go back to sleep and when we wake up later, I'll show you how dirty you really are."

I snuggled close to his strong, sexy masculine scent, letting it travel to my brain and lull me into a deep, restful sleep.

KB Winters

Chapter 11

Max

Waking up in a strange bed was usually cause for alarm, but with Jana's scent still lingering on my body and in my nostrils, I knew exactly where I was and reached out to her. The bed was cool where she'd slept after I'd made her nearly pass out from her orgasms. I groaned and sat up in her bed. The room was neat except for the evidence of our passion last night and this morning in the form of clothes strewn all over the room and pillows dotting the floor.

I stood and went to the master bathroom to wash up because the smells coming from the kitchen—bacon and coffee—had my stomach standing up to remind me I'd burned more calories than I'd consumed last night. I slipped on the green boxer briefs that hung on a drawer handle and made my way down to the kitchen.

I froze just before I reached the doorway as a male voice sounded. A familiar male voice. I looked around the door and froze at the figure sitting at the small round table smiling brightly up at Jana. "Tate?"

He and Jana froze, but turned their gazes to me. "Big brother! Did you miss me?"

I could've throttled the little fucker, but I missed him too damn much and I was so happy to see him. A scowl was fixed on my face as I stalked to him and Tate's grin faded. "Fucking right I missed you. Get your ass over here." I pulled him to a big, emotional hug. It lasted longer than it probably should have, but this was my fucking brother. "Fuck, it's so good to see you, kid." His shoulders relaxed and I realized he was worried about how I'd receive him.

"It's good to see you too, old man."

"Not too old to kick your ass."

He scoffed. "You and what army?"

"Uncle Sam's," we both answered with similar grins. "Where have you been?"

To his credit, Tate's expression straightened, a small smirk still appeared at the corner of his mouth.

"Don't worry, your girl has already given me a proper tongue-lashing about scaring my big bad papa bear."

He sighed but he was serious now. "I needed to decompress for a while and I knew you guys would want to party straight off. I needed to get my head on straight first."

"And before that?" Now that he was okay and free, I wanted some damn answers. "I haven't seen you or talked to you in months, Tate."

He blew out a breath and slipped back into his chair, took a sip of the steaming cup of coffee cradled in his hands. His familiar gray gaze cut to Jana and she gave an encouraging nod. "I needed to make sure the government couldn't use any club business against me."

The words hung in the air between us and I resisted the urge to look at Jana because I couldn't bear to see her wearing an arrogant grin.

Jana broke the contemplative silence "Have a seat," and slid a tall stack of pancakes on the table, then eggs and bacon and fruit.

"How did you find me?" Savior was the only one who knew about Jana and he didn't know her last name.

"Jana called my lawyer."

My head almost swiveled off my shoulders looking to for an explanation.

"I knocked an hour ago and Jana was kind enough to let me in instead of calling the police."

She grinned and blushed prettily. "I figured you probably had enough of them to last you a lifetime. Plus, the resemblance is strong, even with the different hair color." Head down, she kept her focus on the breakfast while Tate and I caught up. "I hope you're not mad, Max. Maybe I shouldn't have interfered, but I knew you were worried about him."

"Mad? I can't believe you did this for me. For us." I couldn't put into words what she meant to me at that moment. I trained my eyes back on him.

"You plan on staying at the compound?"

Tate shook his head. "Nah, I need my own space. I have a hotel stipend for a few weeks so I'll use that while I figure it out."

"Bullshit. I have a spare room. It's only got a bed and a nightstand, but it's yours for however long you want it."

He grinned but I could see the strain it caused. "Thanks, Max."

"I'm just so fucking happy you're out, man."

"Me, too." He smiled and for a moment I caught a glimpse of the boy he used to be before life had shown him what an unfair bitch she could be.

"Eat," Jana insisted, "or I'll start to believe you prefer prison food to mine."

Tate laughed and it was genuine this time. "Yes ma'am. And if I'd gotten food this good in prison, it wouldn't have been so bad." He ate quickly and I could see a restless, unsettled quality that hadn't been there before. "Would you like me to help with something?"

Jana frowned and shook her head. "No. You're a guest."

"Uninvited," he added with a bit of anger.

Jana wasn't fazed though, she turned big green eyes up at him and arched a brow. "That's still a guest." They were locked in a stare down and I didn't know if I should intervene or not.

But Tate relaxed. "Okay then. Thanks for breakfast, Jana. It was nice to meet you."

"You too, Tate. And I'm happy you got your freedom back. Glad I can tell you in person."

He blinked, uncomfortable for a moment with her words but then I saw acceptance dawn. "Thanks. Me, too."

The moment was so tender, so intimate I felt like an outsider and he was my brother. What the fuck was wrong with me? "I'll walk you out." I took a quick detour to hand off my house keys. "Use whatever you like, except my underwear and my condoms."

Tate flashed a grin. "I'm all set in that regard, thanks."

"You need cash?"

He shook his head. "No. What I need is someone who can go through my bank statements. Even though I've been cleared of the crime, the government isn't willing to give up the money they confiscated from me. It's a lot of fucking money, Max."

I sighed, knowing that my morning plans with Jana were about to be derailed. Again. "Come on back in, you should talk to Jana. If she can't help, she can point you in the right direction."

"What? That little bitty thing in the kitchen?"

I grinned and followed behind him. "That little bitty thing is an accountant."

"No shit? How'd you find her?"

"Art therapy."

He looked over his shoulder with a quickly fading grin. "Shit, for real?"

"Yep."

"You doing better?"

"A bit, not much. You?"

Tate shrugged. "Only time will tell." He turned in the doorway and froze. "I think you should've told your girl I was still here."

I peeked over his shoulder to find Jana scrambling off the counter, butt naked, as she tried to cover herself with a kitchen towel and then an apron. "Shit! I thought...never mind. I need a minute, or a million, maybe just a rock to climb under."

I grinned at her adorable awkwardness and Tate laughed. "We'll be in the living room. Tate needs an accountant."

She peeked up over the counter and grinned. "Really? Great! Just…go away please and thanks." She sank back behind the counter, whispering curses to herself. She was so fucking adorable.

"We're in the living room," I told her when Tate fell onto the couch, stifling a laugh. "Don't embarrass her," I warned.

Tate held his hands up in surrender. "Embarrass? I'm jealous as fuck there's no beautiful woman waiting for me butt naked on a counter somewhere. I've been in prison for six years, dude."

"You up for a party tonight?"

"Nope. Dinner?"

"You cooking?"

He shook his head. "You're buying, big brother."

"Gladly." I meant it too. Now that Tate was back where he belonged, maybe I could finally move forward with my life.

KB Winters

Chapter 12

Jana

"You know how to cook?" I stood in my kitchen on Saturday afternoon, leaning against the counter while Max unpacked two paper sacks filled with groceries.

"Damn right I know how to cook, woman. How do you think I survived all these years?"

I grinned at his affronted look. "Aren't there guys whose only job is to feed you?" I bit back a laugh but the more offended he looked the funnier it was.

"Wait until you eat it before commenting." He puffed his chest out, broad shoulders taking up more room than necessary in my small kitchen. "You'll not only love it, you'll beg for the recipe." He was so self-assured I felt my pussy tighten in anticipation.

"I guess we'll see, won't we?" Pushing off the counter, I went over to what could, generously, be called my wet bar. Really it was a hutch topped with bottles, and a drawer full of other cocktail-making tools. "Can you at least tell me what we're having so I can make us drinks?"

"Fish."

I tapped my chin, fully aware of his gaze on me, and thought about what I could make. For a guy like Max it had to pack a punch but it couldn't be too girly. "You're not really a martini kind of guy and a V&T is too plain when I've got a handsome man cooking me dinner."

"Just make something, woman."

I grinned at him the smile he sent back nearly buckled my knees. I loved it when Max smiled; it took the years of pain and war from his face, leaving nothing but a handsome carefree man. "I have just the drink," I told him with a smile and started gathering ingredients.

"You're a great cook and a bartender, why?"

I shrugged even though I knew what he was really asking. "A delicious meal can only be enhanced by the right cocktail." It was a flippant answer and I could hear his frustrated sigh behind me. "You know why."

"Seriously? Because of that fucking scar?"

I finished squeezing the grapefruit and turned to him, pleading with him to understand. "Yes, because of the scar. You have no idea what it means to me that you're not bothered by it, but everyone else is. It's easier, for me, to avoid being made a freak show whenever I leave the house."

He said nothing for a long time and though I felt a twinge of disappointment that he hadn't immediately jumped to tell me I wasn't a freak show, I appreciated that he didn't lie just to make me feel better. "People are assholes."

I grinned and reached for the rimming salt. "Yes, they are. Now you know my secret. Teddy forces me out once a week. Though I'm sure she'd love to get her way more often, it's just easier this way." And cowardly, but sometimes I just had to be a coward.

"I want to take you out again, Jana. You're beautiful and I want to show you a good time."

"You have been showing me the best time, Max. And I'm not just talking about in the bedroom. Or on the counter." I grinned, suddenly distracted by all the deliciously wicked sex I'd been having with the handsome biker. "The point is, we do have a good time. I don't need fancy restaurants and I certainly don't need to be pointed at and whispered about."

"So the assholes win?"

"No, I do. They point and stare and then they get bored, but I don't forget their words so easily. It's not easy to finish a meal after that." Or sleep, or eat for the next few days. "I'm sorry that's not what you wanted to hear."

The constant chopping had stopped and he let out a long, frustrated sigh. "It's just, hell Jana, you deserve more than this."

"Thanks, Max. It means a lot to hear you say that." It did. No one in my life but Teddy had ever thought I deserved anything good. Certainly not Robert Sanborn, who thought I deserved whatever he wanted to give to me, or Karen, whose betrayal had stung even more. "Are we done with this topic?"

"For now."

I finished making the drinks and turned, stopping dead in my tracks at the sight before me. Max stood tall and capable, his jacket gone to reveal a tight gray tee that gave his eyes a more menacing glint that I found endlessly sexy. Each time he moved his muscles bunched and flexed, back muscles popping out as he stirred vegetables, brows dipped low as he carefully seasoned two thick filets of white fish. "I've never watched a man cook before. It's kind of erotic."

He froze, just his head swiveled to meet my gaze. "Dirty hands and raw fish turn you on?"

I licked my lips. "Watching your body move while you cook is totally turning me on. Cocktail?"

He nodded, a dark sexy twinkle lit his gaze as I walked the icy drink over to him. "Dirty hands," he said when I handed him the drink.

"Of course." Two could play this game. I hoped. The rim of the glass touched his lips and I tilted it, my gaze focused first on that plump bottom lip as it curved under the rim of the cup, the length of his neck and the way his Adam's apple bobbed when he swallowed, was hypnotic. I couldn't look away. It was completely erotic.

Max gripped my wrist with his food-covered hands and I slowly moved the glass from his mouth. "Jana," he growled in a hot, dark sound that shot straight to my pussy.

"What?" I licked my lips, staring at his.

"You're killin' me," he groaned and pressed me against the fridge using nothing but his body, slamming his mouth against mine, a hot, swirling whirlwind of sensations shooting through me. The cool stainless steel fridge against my back, the soft, slightly salty taste of his tongue, the feel of his big hand cupping my breast and pinching my nipple. But his mouth and his tongue were his preferred torture instruments, slicking across my tongue in a tempting tornado that had my hands shooting out to him for purchase.

His cock grew hard behind his jeans and I wanted him. Right here and now, so I jumped into his arms, growling at the feel of his big hands gripping my ass. "Max."

His hands slid under my shirt, cool and slightly slimy from the food. "Oh, shit," he spat out and seconds later the smoke alarm sounded. "Fuck. See how you distract me?"

I grinned. "Little ol' me?"

He shot me a look that made us both laugh. "You should probably get changed," he said and I glanced down, bursting out with a loud laugh at the sight of his sticky, food covered handprints all over my shirt and jeans.

"What a handsy chef you are," I joked.

"What a tempting treat you are," he shot back, his gaze as hot as ever.

I swallowed feeling turned on beyond all reason as an idea struck. "I'm going to turn that off," I yelled over the increasing shrill tone of the alarm before I climbed on the counter and took it off the mount. "And I'm going to go get changed. Be back in a bit."

"Take your time," he groused. "I have to start over."

"We could always order in," I offered.

"No. Go change. I'm cooking, dammit."

I grinned and made my way to the shower with a smile I couldn't erase. Being with Max was easy. He was honest, bluntly so, which meant I didn't have to worry about what he said. The sex was unbelievable and I was pretty sure I was addicted to his body. To him. Which meant a quick shower only made me want another set of hands all over me. Max's.

I lathered mounds of body butter all over my skin, spritzed perfume in my hair and all over my breasts before I headed downstairs. "How long until dinner," I called out from the middle of the staircase.

"Half hour or so," he called back sounding more relaxed than he had twenty minutes ago.

Perfect. I crept down the stairs and stood in the doorway, watching him move around the kitchen, so graceful and athletic. And for the moment, he was all mine. "Max."

He turned and instantly his gaze was lit with fire. "Fuck, Jana." He stalked to me, food all but forgotten.

"I hope you set the timer because I want you in me. Right now."

"Where," he growled a moment before he reached me, hands gripping my waist and pulling me close.

"Wherever you want me."

He growled and picked me up, set me on the edge of the counter and buried his head between my legs. Licking and lapping until my thighs trembled with the pleasure trying to break free of my body. "I can't get enough of you," he growled, making my nipples harden to painful points.

"Good, because as much as I love the way you eat my pussy, I need your big cock pounding into me and I need it now."

He reared back, shooting me a dark look as he quickly removed his pants and boxer briefs. In one quick move he had a condom on and he was lowering me onto his thick, hard prick. "Fuck!"

He froze as I pulsed around him. "Max, move. Fuck me."

He gripped my ass and turned, smacking my back against the wall but I didn't care because he began to move hard and fast, short, hard strokes that plunged the depths of me until I couldn't see or breathe anything that wasn't Max. Over and over his cock slid in deep, punishing strokes that gave me more pleasure than I'd ever felt. His teeth sank into a breast and his hips took over with a mind of their own, moving as though powered by an engine and moments later I was shouting my pleasure into the quiet house, pulsing around him as he continued fucking me hard and fast.

"Yes, Max! More. Just like...that!" The final wave of orgasm pulled me under and took Max with it, my name a thunderous growl on his lips. "I feel like I should be cooking *you* dinner," I told him breathlessly.

"Believe me, that was worth a week of dinners."

I grinned, my heart feeling so full and my body so satisfied that I ignored the warning bells that were a distant clang in my mind. "Well, let's see if I can bump that up to a month of dinners."

He grinned and leaned forward just as the oven timer sounded. "Let's pick this up for dessert."

"I guess now I know why I made the fresh whipped cream." His gaze darkened and I knew I was in trouble, but it was the best trouble of my life.

***

Over the next few weeks, Max and I settled into a comfortable routine. He spent his nights with me. Mostly. Every night, after we fell into an exhausted sleep after making love, he slipped out before the sun came up. I hated it mostly because I loved waking up with his big arms wrapped around me, but it'd been so long since that happened that I could barely remember it. It fell into the category of another thing I wouldn't get to experience, and that just fucking sucked.

I understood Max's desire to keep me safe, and his very genuine fears that he had about his nightmares and post-traumatic stress, but I still hated it. I hated feeling like my first relationship was a half relationship—or worse—a dirty little secret. Especially when I knew this wasn't some illicit affair, he was my man. That was already something I didn't think I'd ever have, yet here I was already wanting more. Being greedy.

And maybe I was being greedy, but the thing was, if I had to settle for less, I'd rather be alone.

But the biggest problem, I admitted to myself as I stared at the sushi menu I was using to avoid having a conversation with Teddy, was that after a month straight of seeing each other, dating and fucking, it made me feel cheap that he would just sneak out of my bed in the middle of the night. It felt like we were doing something wrong, or like *he thought* we were doing something wrong. It felt even worse when combined with his surprise date last week. In a public place.

I hated it and it only made me angry since we'd talked about this before—more than once—and I made my feelings clear. But I bit my tongue, not wanting to rock the boat. Okay, and not wanting to give up the amazing physical benefits of my relationship with Max. But it really was becoming problematic, so I agreed to lunch at the new German-themed Sushi Haus because I needed expert advice. "So, tell me oh wise one, what should I do?"

Teddy tapped her long, French-manicured nails on the table, her eagle-eyed gaze burning a hole through me. "Talk to Max. Tell him how you feel."

Yeah, that was easy for Teddy to say. The woman never met a confrontation she didn't face head on. "And if how I feel doesn't matter?" Which, let's be honest, was my biggest fear.

She shrugged her delicate shoulders with a casual grace I envied. "Then you have to decide how important it is to you, and maybe how important he is." Teddy sighed and I could feel her sympathy radiating off her. "I can't tell you what to do Jana, but you deserve it all, the same as the rest of us. If he can't give you what you need, maybe it's time to move on."

Move on. *Move on?* I couldn't do that. Not only because I had no idea where to start a thing like that, but also because I was pretty sure that I was—or already had—fallen in love with the idiot. But, Teddy was right. I needed to figure out if I could accept everything about him. "What if I can't accept it? Can I try to change it?" That was the great thing about accounting; the numbers didn't lie, but loopholes meant you could change things around until they looked how you wanted them to look.

Teddy arched a sculpted red brow, her beautiful face a study in skepticism. "Honey, we always think we can change them. We can't."

I nodded, waiting for the young waiter to drop off our food, as I thought about her words. I'd read tons of books and magazines on relationships. I'd overheard girls talk about changing men, but it was different with Max. He had PTSD, a real, diagnosed problem. PTSD could be treated with therapy and meds. And time. Avoidance wouldn't do anything to fix it, and that's what Max was doing. "Can I encourage him to attend more therapy?"

Teddy shook her head, obstinance written all over her expression. "No. Hell no, absolutely not." She tilted her head my way and smiled. "Well you can suggest it, but if he shuts you down, then you have your answer. Don't push."

Well shit, that wasn't at all what I wanted to hear. But, I supposed that meant it was just what I needed to hear. "Thanks, Teddy. I think I'll take that cocktail now."

"Sake?" she asked with a cheeky grin.

I glared at her. "A *real* drink, smart ass." She laughed and I joined in, happy at the ease with which we could go from serious topics to silly. "What's new with you?"

Her face lit up the way it always did when she talked about work. Teddy saw men, dated them, but she never got involved. They never made her smile, other than in amusement at them, but it wasn't the same. "With the wedding from hell behind me and bringing me more business, I'm feeling better. Especially with two newly rich reality stars who want lavish 'Vegas, Baby' weddings. They're nice, down to earth and out of their depth. They are absolutely adorable, so I have nothing to complain about," she said, sounding a tad pissed about that fact. "Oh, and someone recognized me at the Wynn."

Uh oh, I knew Teddy hated it when she was recognized from the decade she spent as one of the most sought after models in the world. People, complete strangers, were quick to tell her how pretty she still was as though somehow that was a compliment. And I knew how she seethed over her least favorite sentence in the English language. *Too bad about the leg, but you're still hot.* "I'm sorry, Teddy. Was he nice, at least?" These days, *that* would be considered an improvement.

"It was a woman, actually. She had big dreams of being a model as a kid, just like me. But after seeing what happened to me, she decided to skip it altogether. She's in town for some big conference as the keynote speaker."

I laughed. "Your life is completely unbelievable. Let me guess, she invited you to attend?"

"If I want to," she added reluctantly. "I might go. I mean, she dodged a bullet I ran toward at full speed, and she did it because of me. It feels like it balances out the shitty karma scale. Or something."

I repeated her words with a smile. "Want to get out of here and have some real cocktails?"

"Do you even have to ask?" She was on her feet as she pulled cash from her purse and left it on the table. I did the same and left the tip before following her out, ignoring the few people who found my face more interesting than their lunch. I ignored them and rushed outside.

I drove us home as I always did, because driving allowed me to decide when I left anywhere. I needed that control and I didn't give a damn how it looked to the outside world. I drove a little faster than necessary and kicked my shoes off the moment I stepped inside. My whole body relaxed, and I was ready for a drink. "Gin, grapefruit and mint?"

"You had me at gin," Teddy joked and kicked off her red stilettos before she dropped into a kitchen chair. "Have you thought anymore about that art show?"

"I have and I think I'm going to do it. But Moon wants a series of at least five and I'm working out an idea in my head." I had the idea clearly defined but I wasn't brave enough to ask the subjects, especially Teddy. "I'll figure it out."

"You always do, Jana."

I smiled at Teddy's words, but they stayed with me long after she'd gone. I always figured it out because I had to, there was no one else to figure it out for me.

KB Winters

Chapter 13

Max

"Are you still seeing your lady friend?"

Dr. Singh had put his notepad down as he looked at me, hands resting in his lap. The picture of calm.

I smiled at his old-fashioned term and nodded. "I am, and things are going well." They were going well, but over the past week I had a feeling that Jana was having doubts. About me or us, I didn't know.

"And the nightmares?"

I sighed and let my body sink into the plush leather chair. "Yeah, they're still going on. But I have it under control." I stayed with Jana until she was deep asleep and oblivious to the sounds I made as I got dressed and went home. It was the best option, giving me some time with her in bed before the nightmares returned.

"Are you letting her help with them?"

I didn't want to tell him the truth, but this was fucking therapy. "She doesn't see them. I go home after she's asleep. Jana doesn't need to deal with my bullshit."

He let out a deep sigh and flashed a smile tinged with disappointment. "We'll talk more about this next week, but just do me a favor Max, okay?"

I nodded and motioned for him to continue.

"Imagine how Jana feels. You presumably have sex with her and then sneak out in the middle of the night."

"Dammit, Doc." I stood and shook his hand, ignoring the amused smirk he wore as I left his office. His words wouldn't leave my mind as I hopped on my bike and made my way to Mayhem Burger where I was meeting Tate. He was still staying at my house and keeping his distance from the club, for some reason. But he wanted to talk, and I would be there.

We'd already lost too many years.

Tate was already in a black and white checkered booth when I arrived, sipping a beer and looking casual as fuck, not at all like a man who'd spent six years in prison. "Hey man, what's up? Haven't seen much of you."

He smiled up at me, reminding me so much of the kid who used to run around trying to do everything I did. "You've been occupied by a beautiful woman, that's why." He smirked and shrugged. "My attorneys officially filed the lawsuit today against the cops and the prosecutor. They fucking owe me, Max. They stole years from me and they knew, fucking knew, I didn't do a damn thing."

He seethed, his blonde hair and golden looks darkened in anger. He was still angry and I didn't fucking blame him. Hell, I was still angry for him.

"All I can do now is fuck them the way they fucked me." He smacked his fist on the table between us to punctuate his anger while I asked a passing waitress for two more beers.

"And two shots," I told her with a smile before turning back to Tate. "I'm with you. Whatever you need."

Tate nodded and sat silently browsing the menu until we both placed our orders—double fucking bacon cheeseburgers with steak fries—and he turned to me. "I need you to keep the club off my fucking back. I'll deal with them when I'm ready, but right now I need to fight this shit. I have to, Max."

"You got it. What else?" I didn't bother telling him that both Cross and Savior had been asking about him and wondering where in the hell he'd been.

"Your girl invited me to dinner," he said without preamble.

I froze as his words sank in and I felt an irrational anger rise up in me, but also shock. "She did *what*?"

Tate shrugged like it was no big deal. "Said in case I wanted to talk about something that wasn't my time in prison and enjoy a good meal. She's nice, bro. You could do a lot worse than her." The waitress placed our burgers in front of us and Tate dug in like he hadn't had a decent meal in, well six goddamn years.

I still didn't like the idea of Jana inviting my brother to dinner. Maybe it was jealousy or maybe it was something else, something darker that burned in my gut, but I fucking hated that she went to my brother behind my back. It was one thing that she called when he got out of prison. But even back then she didn't tell me. Now this? It made me wonder if I could trust her. I didn't like secrets. Not from her. "You don't even know her," I argued pointlessly.

Tate frowned and looked at me like I'd grown two heads. "No, I don't. Then again, no one else has offered to talk about shit other than the six years of my life that I lost. Or how I'm gonna 'get paid' and all that shit. Is it so wrong that one person on this fucking planet is treating me like a human instead of a statistic?" He was angry and I deserved it, but I was fucking angry too.

"No, guess not. Do what you want."

Tate barked out a laugh and smiled. "You're seriously jealous? You are fucked in the head, Max. She is doing this because of you, dumbass."

That was bullshit and we both knew it. "Yeah? Tell me, how does a dinner that doesn't include me have any fucking thing to do with me?" I stared, waiting for an answer as he took bite after bite of his burger and fries, enjoying the meal the way a man fresh from prison could.

"I'm important to you and she's offering me something I need, because she thinks it would help you. That's just my guess though since I've been locked up and I don't have a woman who gives two shits about me. So hey, what the fuck do I know?" He stood, looking disgusted as hell as he shook his head.

"Thanks for lunch. Catch you later, Max." Tate walked away, leaving me sitting there like a damn fool.

How was I the bad guy when it was my fucking girl inviting another man to her home for dinner? This day had gone from bad to worse, and the fucking sun hadn't even set yet.

***

I knew it wasn't a dream but that didn't mean I could do shit to stop it. I could still smell the scent of sex and Jana's flowery perfume and knew it didn't belong in the goddamn desert but the convoy was just moments away from shit going tits up and my heart raced as sweat beaded on my forehead, slid down my back. The sun was hot, burning fucking hot, at least one hundred and twenty degrees and no shade around for miles.

Then it happened. We hit the half-mile marker to our second to last destination where we would each undergo a lengthy debriefing about the mission. Then we would all be headed stateside for a nice long break. But instead of detailed questions and answers, we hit a fucking roadside bomb and then there was chaos as the vehicle flipped on its side, the loud explosion and sounds of crunching metal drowned out everything for long seconds as I struggled to see right in front of my eyes. As the smoke began to clear, along with my hearing, the sounds of several brothers screaming in pain came in loud and clear.

I crawled on my hands and knees behind the transport vehicle and aimed beyond the smoke, in the direction of incoming fire. I yelled but no words came out, and worse, no one answered. When my gun was empty, I reloaded and emptied it again, and again until I was out of ammo. The fucking shooting never stopped so I quickly crawled to a fallen brother, grabbing his weapon and ammo before taking cover behind the overturned vehicle again.

I knew what happened next. I'd had this dream enough times to know a pair of black feet would appear in the smoke, moving closer. But this time I wouldn't just wake up, I'd fight the fucker. I had the ammo so I squeezed the trigger but, goddammit, it wasn't hitting him so I dropped the gun and charged. I usually woke up at this point so I didn't know what the fuck to do but wrap my hands around his neck and squeezed even though I couldn't see his face. I could only feel his hands smacking and scratching at my arms.

"Max, please. Let go. It's me. It's Jana."

I heard the voice and felt the small, delicate hands squeezing my arms, scratching at me but I couldn't stop.

"Max! Let go, Max!" Fingernails sliced through my arm and I squeezed harder. "Max, please!"

It was that tearful plea that pulled me from a sleeping nightmare and into a real life, waking nightmare.

"Jana!"

My eyes adjusted to the semi-darkness and all I could see was her red, tear-stained face, big brown eyes filled with fear and sympathy.

"Jana, shit. What the fuck?" I sat on top of her, my hands wrapped around the delicate slope of her neck. I was off her in an instant, chest heaving as horror ripped through me.

"Shit. Goddammit! I'm sorry."

"It's okay," she said softly, her voice shaky with tears. "Are you all right, Max?"

"I should be asking you that. Shit, Jana, I could've killed you." And my own hands shook as that reality settled over me like a hot flame. "Shit, I could have fucking killed you."

"But you didn't, Max. Is this still happening every night?" How could she sit there and look at me like that, brown eyes filled with concern for me, instead of herself.

It caused a squeezing sensation in my chest but it also pissed me off. "Don't worry about me, Jana. Worry about yourself."

She flinched at my words. "Don't tell me what I can care or worry about, Max. Is this why you don't stay the night?"

"What do *you* think?" I had my jeans on but unfastened, arms crossed as I looked at her.

"I think this is bullshit. Is this how you plan to live your life, Max?" The plea in her voice nearly undid me, but I had to stay strong. No matter what.

"What difference does it make? This is why I don't stay here, Jana. I'm trying to protect you!"

She shook her head, swinging her legs over the edge of the bed and stood, completely unashamed of her nudity. Even as anger and terror seared the blood in my veins, I couldn't help but appreciate her form. Short with curves for days, she was a gorgeous woman, but the sight of those dusky raspberry nipples made my mouth water. And I knew I needed to leave. "Bullshit. You're trying to protect yourself, Max. I can't do anything but accept it."

Suddenly her anger and frustration were gone. Worry still darkened her deep brown eyes but her shoulders fell as though she was giving up. "That's all I'm asking you to do, dammit."

She gave a short nod, looking like a wounded damn puppy as she slipped into the bathroom and locked the door behind her. I should've waited for her to come out so we could discuss this like adults, but I couldn't. Thoughts of how close I'd come to genuinely hurting her had me quickly dressing and rushing through the front door without a look back.

I hopped on my bike and went home, calling Dr. Singh to see if he could fit me in for an emergency session. I needed space to figure my shit out, so I packed a bag, hopped on my bike and drove until my eyes were too heavy to keep going.

I woke up a few hours later and did it all over again.

Chapter 14

Jana

After spending the day doing quarterly reports for several clients, I snuck in a quick workout and then got busy on the dinner I wanted to cook for Max. After radio silence for a full week, he'd finally called to say he wanted to talk. Though I was upset that he'd vanished after the weirdest morning of my life, I agreed that we needed to talk. I'd gotten fresh seafood from the market so I decided to mix it up with paella and grilled sardines with a Greek salad. It wasn't fancy but it was hearty and I was starving. And if this thing went sideways, I'd have lots of food to feed a broken heart.

As I got dressed though, I couldn't help but think about my conversation with Teddy. I knew that time was running out and I would have to say something to Max. My hands shook at the idea of things ending between us. I didn't want that to happen, but something had to change.

When Max rang the bell, I pulled it open with a smile, only to be met with a half-smile, half-scowl and a half-hearted greeting.

"Hey," I finally said as all the anticipation inside of me deflated. It became clear as I poured the sangria that this night wasn't going to go the way I thought it would. I cranked the heat on the stove from a low simmer to a straight up boil to speed things along. "Ready to eat?"

"I could eat." His voice was blanked of all emotion, like a robot had replaced the man I thought I knew.

Something was definitely going on and if I were a betting woman, I'd say it had something to do with me. Or more accurately, with us. I felt the air shift when he came into the kitchen, but I didn't turn, instead listening as he pulled out a chair and dropped down into it. "How are you, Max?"

"I'm fine, Jana. You?"

I sighed and gave a mumbled, "Fine." I was a woman who knew when to cut her losses and tonight counted as a lost fucking cause. When the food was ready, I plated it up and left the sardines on a large plate because there was no way in hell I would sit through a painfully silent meal I'd spent the better part of an hour preparing.

"Let's eat and watch a movie," I told him, taking the sardines, napkins and flatware into the living room without waiting for an answer.

Max said nothing, just grabbed the glasses along with the rest of the sangria and took a seat on the middle cushion of the sofa.

With a big sigh, I found a shoot 'em up movie on Netflix and put it on, getting lost in my own head as I ate. Gunshots provided the perfect soundtrack for my tumultuous thoughts, which were mostly centered on the man beside me. Clearly Max hadn't been sleeping well because each time I saw him, the dark circles under his eyes were a darker shade of purple. Today they were practically black, yet he said nothing.

"You want more?"

I looked at him holding the sardines and shook my head. "All yours." By the time the movie was over, my hunger wasn't sated and all the excitement and anticipation I'd built up at seeing Max again had vanished. Tonight, I actually wanted him to go home. Now. "Are you staying here tonight?"

I knew before he even answered, based on the tense set of his shoulders and the way his jaw clenched. And based on the past month or more of experience.

"Nah, I have to be up early tomorrow for some stuff."

Stuff. Right. I stood and grabbed the plates, stacking them and taking them to the kitchen. I returned for the rest, leaving my own glass and pitcher right where it was, because I had a feeling I'd finish it off before bed. Max hadn't moved so I decided against using the dishwasher, instead filling the sink with hot soapy water and plunging my hands deep into it. There weren't many to do but I took my time, trying to get my anger and frustration under control. Exploding at Max would do nothing to solve this issue between us, never mind what his other issue was today.

"What are you doing in here?"

"The dishes."

"Why?"

I sighed and turned. "Who else is going to do them, Max? I live alone."

"I'm leaving."

"I heard you the first time."

He sighed. The sound of his footsteps grew closer until the heat of his body began to envelop mine. "What is this, Jana?"

"Nothing. Look, you said you have to be up early so you should probably get going. Do you need coffee to make sure you're okay to drive?"

"No, I don't need fucking coffee. Just tell me what the hell is going on?"

His hands landed on my shoulder and I tensed, even though I wanted to lean into him, feel the hot, hard heat of his body. But I couldn't. Nothing felt right anymore and I just wanted to cry.

"Nothing is going on with me, Max. You showed up when clearly you didn't want to be here and now you have to get up early, so I'll see you whenever."

"What the hell does that mean?" His voice roared in my small kitchen, making me jump.

"It means it doesn't fucking matter, Max." I pulled the drain on the water and turned. "Good night."

My pulse raced as I looked up at him, those big gray eyes dark as gun metal and as intense as a hurricane. I loved him, but a love like this might kill me. He stared at me for a long time before he nodded, turned on his heels and left.

I changed into a long t-shirt that came just below my knees before curling up on the sofa with the rest of my sangria. Reality came crashing down at the bottom of the third glass. I thought Max and I were building something, working toward a real relationship. But we weren't. We were nothing more than two people who spent time together and fucked. That was it. Now that I knew that painful truth, I had an even harder decision to make.

Could I live in this half of a relationship where Max slipped out of my bed each night and went home to face his demons alone? I'd have killed for someone other than an overworked social worker to help me deal with the trauma of my scars. Yet here I was, not enough.

Again.

As my eyelids grew heavy, the answer skated on the outer edges of my consciousness. I might not be the prettiest girl around, or the smartest. But I did have some self-respect left.

Mostly.

But what did self-respect matter when you were facing heartbreak for the very first time?

***

"Everything looks good as far as bookkeeping, but I noticed you aren't taking advantage of every deduction you could, and I've put it in my notes so you can think about it."

I sat across from Mr. Cross inside my office, dressed like a professional in plain black pants and a black blouse, doing my best not to notice how much…man he was. Not that I was interested in him like that, but the man had a presence that was hard to ignore. He was big, really big, at least six and a half feet with the body of a linebacker. I imagined he wasn't a man who had a hard time with the ladies. But he was a client and those thoughts were totally inappropriate.

"Otherwise, Mr. Cross, your business is thriving. Congratulations."

He grinned a sheepish sort of grin that showed off oddly boyish dimples and he scraped a hand over his short chocolate-colored hair.

"Thanks, and it's just Cross. Ms. Carter."

"Jana, please," I said automatically because it was good to keep things semi-formal when handling people's money.

"Do you have any questions?"

He shook his head and I stood to lead him out of the house when I remembered one final thing. "Have you considered taking advantage of the green tourism with shirts and bags and other things people might want as souvenirs they can actually take home with them?"

He blinked and stood. "I hadn't, but I'll have the guys look into it. Thank you again, Ms., uh, Jana."

"No problem," I told him as I pulled open the door and offered up a hand to shake. "I'll send updates quarterly and call if anything sends up any alarm bells, okay?"

"Sounds good. Thanks again."

"What the fuck is going on here?"

I startled at the sound of Max's angry voice and turned to see his nostrils flaring and spitting out fire.

He was spoiling for a fight. I clenched my jaws and smiled at Mr. Cross. "You'll have to forgive my friend, apparently he's forgotten his manners."

"Don't worry about it, Jana. Thanks for your help." He gave a wave but he didn't move and I felt like something was happening that I didn't quite understand.

"My brother wasn't enough? What are you, some fucking down low biker bunny?"

I sucked in a breath, and in that moment, I completely understood what people meant when they said their heart broke in half. Nothing in my life, not the attack by Robert nor the greater betrayal of Karen, not even the death of my parents had hurt as much as this. Because I was too young to remember, but now it felt like a small favor. Max's eyes were filled with disgust, his voice dripping with hate. Mr. Cross stood between us and I tried to push him aside. "Mr. Cross, please, don't get involved. I'm fine."

He ignored me, glaring down at Max because as big as Max was, he was bigger. "What the fuck is your problem with me and why are you talking to Ms. Carter like that?" A giant hand landed on Max's chest and he moved back a step.

"Ms.? Why the fuck are you calling her Ms. Carter?"

Mr. Cross frowned down at him, blue eyes as dark and angry as Max's gray ones. "It's her name asshole, and generally how people address those they have professional relationships with. Asshole."

Max blinked once. Twice. And I could see the moment it had all become clear because his shoulders deflated all the anger out of him, but he didn't seem at all contrite. "Oh. Why didn't you say anything?"

Ugh, men. I shook my head and turned on my heels, slamming the door behind me. Max was a jerk and I was the idiot who'd gone and fallen for the first guy to show me a little honest attention. As angry as I was, as much as Max's words had hurt me, I was angrier with myself. I let myself believe that I could have something normal, something fun and light and hot. I should've known better.

Life had forced the lesson down my throat enough times.

I stopped in my office to save the documents again and shut down my computer for the day as the bell rang out front. Ignoring it was easy enough since I knew who it would be, but just to make it easier I went into my bedroom to change and cranked up the music. I could still hear the bell, just barely so I turned up the volume again and made my way to the kitchen.

Cooking wasn't just a necessity; it was a great way to channel excess energy while I thought through problems, whether professional or personal. Admittedly, though there hadn't been many personal problems in my life, many a professional conundrum had been resolved in my tiny kitchen. By the time I'd completely scaled the trout, the knocking and ringing had stopped.

But I kept the music on high just in case. Fish and steamed veggies wasn't exactly exotic cuisine, but the Pina Colada turned it into a culinary party for one.

That didn't sound pathetic at all.

Chapter 15

Max

Drinking to drown one's sorrows was a young man's game, and I hadn't been young since I was eighteen. The nights were long and cold, and lonely as fuck, and the days were even worse because everything looked normal and bright and happy. When it shouldn't. Because things weren't. Things were shit.

I'd fucked up big with Jana and it was looking like she might not forgive me, at least if I went by how steadfastly she ignored my calls and my texts, and me in general. She wouldn't answer the door, even when her car was there, and no matter how often I stopped by, I couldn't catch her coming or going. What I didn't understand was that she seemed more upset about how I'd acted in front of Cross than the fact that my fucked up brain had nearly killed her. That didn't make sense, but I didn't care, I kept trying. And failing.

So, I waited until Friday, until art class.

Only she wasn't there and thirty minutes in, she hadn't shown up and I knew she wouldn't. The instructor, Moon, gave me a pitying smile that I hated as I stood up to leave, fed up with this whole fucking week. "She's probably just taking the week off to finish up her series for the show."

I looked at Moon, dressed in a long blue velvet dress, Birkenstock sandals and an arm full of copper bangles. She looked like a sorceress or something. "What show?"

She frowned and a wariness appeared in her gaze that I didn't like. "It's nothing really, just a few artists I've asked to donate their work to my next show." She reached behind me and handed me a purple sheet of paper. "I hope to see you there."

"Maybe," I told her as I looked at the details and noted the date was just over a month away. "Thanks, Moon."

"You're very welcome, Max. I hope this class has helped you in some way."

I offered up a smile at her sincere words and the hope shining in her eyes. In a way, the class had helped because it was where I met Jana, who had done a lot for me. But that's not what she meant. "It has, Moon. Thanks." With ten minutes before class ended, I rushed out to the street and hopped on my bike in a hurry to get home. Where pizza and cold beer waited.

Throw in a little Netflix and I had the perfect night. *Perfectly pathetic.* It wasn't how I'd spent my Friday nights lately and the contrast was killing me. Everything was so fucked up and it was all my fault. Well, not *all* my fault. Jana had to own some of the blame too since she'd invited Tate to dinner and then had taken a job with my club. I couldn't quite figure out why she would do that and not tell me because I'd been sleeping for shit lately, which meant I was beyond exhausted and unfocused.

I'd given up on thinking about Jana after a while because I just couldn't take it. I put on an old sitcom that I'd missed while I was overseas and drank too much beer. Enough beer to dull the memory of how

Jana had looked when I accused her of fucking my brother and the club President, or the fear when my hands were clasped around her throat. There wasn't enough beer in all of Mayhem, hell in all of Nevada.

Around ten the door opened and Tate made a shit ton of noise as he came inside carrying a paper bag that smelled like home cooking. "I guess you already ate," he grinned. "Guess I'll eat this later."

"What is it?" I looked over my shoulder at him, trying to get a look at the bag. "Where were you?"

Tate rolled his eyes. "Dinner. Steak nachos. It was damn delicious and the company was good too. She made too much, she said, but we both know she just wanted to make sure you were eating. Not that you deserve it."

I couldn't argue that point even though it did make my lips curl to hear proof that she felt as fucked up as I did. "She's better off," I told him even though I didn't believe it.

"If you say so." But he laid me bare with a gaze that told me he knew I was lying to myself. "I'll just put this in the fridge for later then."

I was off my feet in a hurry, practically chasing my brother into the small, sparse kitchen. "I didn't say I didn't want it. Gimme." I held out my hand and in that moment, I was catapulted back in time and holding my hand in the same way for Tate to give me a toy he'd taken from the corner store. He'd refused and I picked his scrawny ass up and tossed him over my shoulder as I made my way back to the store and Mr. Collazo, the owner who always looked the other way when we were a little short on cash. The memory made me laugh.

"Okay, you've officially lost it. Go talk to Jana and get your shit straightened out." He backed away, purposely looking like he thought I might snap.

I told him about the memory and he laughed. "What a weird thing to remember."

Tate shrugged as he unloaded the bag. "Better than the other memories you're having. Guess that's why you always come home." His words were said without judgment but still, it stung to know anyone had been around during my nightmares.

"Yeah. The nightmares are a bitch, but I'm handling them."

He arched a blonde brow up at me. "You sure? Is this what caused the beef between you and Jana? Because I gotta say, she seems like the supportive type."

"She is, and no it's not."

I told him what I said to her and watched his eyes grow bigger and wider. "Now she's not speaking to me at all, and I don't fucking blame her. But I can't leave her alone." I shook my head, still unable to wrap my mind around everything. "The crazy thing is she's more pissed about this than the fact I nearly choked her in the middle of a nightmare."

My brother stared at me for a long time. For so damn long that I thought maybe I had guacamole on my face as I dug into the nachos. "You're in love with her."

I frowned. "I don't do love other than, you know, mom and you." It was crazy to think that after just a few weeks, okay more like a few months, I could have fallen in love.

"Well then I won't tell you that Jana looks pale and sad, withdrawn. She probably wanted to cancel on me, but she did as promised and gave me an evening of good food and great conversation."

I was still jealous as hell of Tate, but not the way I was when he'd first told me about her invitation. This time, it was because he was welcome and I wasn't. "Yeah I'm glad for you."

He laughed and shook his head like it was the most amusing thing in the world. "You're a terrible liar, but that's okay. I'd be feeling like an asshole too in your position."

"Yeah, thanks," I told his retreating form and turned back to finish off the nachos, wishing I was sitting in Jana's colorful kitchen eating it while the smells of cooking still filled the house. Her sweet smile shining down on me, waiting for me to take that first bite.

"Shit."

I stood and went to get my phone, shooting off a quick text that simply read, "Thanks for the food."

I waited and waited but she never replied.

I felt shitty. Awful. But also proud that she'd stood up for herself.

Too bad it was against me.

I grabbed the bottle of Jack and went to my room to face my demons.

Alone.

***

As soon as my eyes opened—for the second time—I hopped up, showered to wash off the drunken sweats and got dressed. I had only one thing on my agenda for the day and that was getting Jana to talk to me. I owed her an apology, a bigger one than I knew how to give so I hoped simple would do. When I finally left my room, I found Tate already in the kitchen.

"You're up early."

He shook his head. "No, you are. Tough night?"

I shrugged and went for the coffee pot. "You could say that. What are you up to today?"

"Meeting with the lawyers."

"I'm headed to Jana's. I've got to get her to listen to me so we can talk." I shook my head and set the empty mug in the sink. "Listen to me, I sound like a fucking pussy. You spent six years in prison for a crime you didn't commit and I'm bitching about a woman." Disgusted, I looked around for my boots and found them under the kitchen table.

"See? That shit right there, that's why I accepted Jana's offer to dinner. She talked to me, about her boring ass job, her beautiful best friend always trying to make her go out in public and how she misses the parents she can barely remember. She didn't hold back on her shit because of mine. That's what I need."

Shit. "You couldn't have just said that shit? For all my good looks, Tate, I am not a goddamn mind reader. You know how helpless I fucking felt when I came here and found out what happened? I'm your older brother, been protecting you most of my life. Fuck."

"First off, fuck you, I'm the pretty one." He batted his lashes and just like that the tension disappeared and we were both laughing like fools.

"You might be pretty, but I'm the hot one. Everyone knows that."

Another smile curved his lips and he stood. "Well get your hot ass on over to that woman and grovel if you have to. And Max, trust me, you have to."

The drive to Jana's was short, but even obeying every traffic law hadn't delayed my arrival by more than a couple minutes. I sat on my bike until I gathered my thoughts but I knew she had to have heard me drive up. I made the short trip from the curb to her door, only she didn't answer. But her car sat in the driveway, cool to the touch and I knew she was home.

I had a feeling I knew where she would be this time of day with the sun shining but the heat not yet oppressive, and that's where I found her. Enticing figure kneeling on the ground, heart-shaped ass wiggling in the air as she played in the dirt, giving me a long, seductive look at nearly all of her curves. I kept my presence quiet for several long moments so I could just...soak her in. "I'm sorry," I finally blurted out.

Jana froze at the sound of my voice, pushed her hands on the hard earth to spring up to her feet. A scowl had already set on her pretty face, making the long scar an angry shade of red. Clearly, she was unhappy at my unannounced visit. "Don't be, Max. You said what you thought." She slid her sunglasses over her eyes, shielding them from me as she crossed her arms over her chest. There was enough distance between us for me to know just how much my words had hurt her.

"I didn't mean it, though. That's why I'm apologizing. It was anger and jealousy talking." I took a step forward and she didn't budge. "I was an ass and I'm sorry. Forgive me?"

She shook her head, blond tendrils flying loose from the high bun on her head, framing her face like a halo when the sun caught it just right. "No, I don't forgive you Max. Not because I'm mad, because I'm not really. I shouldn't have expected more than the sex, but I think we've run our course." She spoke so calm and quiet, like she'd given this a lot of thought. A lot more than I had if I was being honest.

"Well I don't." I tried to match the calm in her voice but I heard the tension and I knew she did too.

But she shook her head again, this time sending the entire blond bun falling down around her shoulders. "That's because you don't want an actual relationship. You want someone to sleep with who won't make demands of you, and you thought I was that girl. It's not your fault. I thought I was that girl too, willing to accept what I could get. But it turns out, I'm not."

"I can't believe you would say that to me. What have I done to make you think that?"

She scoffed and shook her head. "Really? Okay, let's start with the fact that you never stay the night because heaven forbid I see the pain you're in. You won't even talk about it with me, and there's the fact that you think I'm the kind of woman who would fuck you, your brother and a client of mine. I think that covers it." She grabbed up her gardening tools and dropped them into a large plastic pail.

"So, I'm a bad guy for wanting to protect you?"

"No," she said, a smile ghosting around her lips. "I never said you were a bad guy, because I think you're one of the good ones. But I don't think I'm the woman for you."

"Why?"

"Because if I were you'd understand my desire to want to help and protect you too. But you don't, and that's okay Max."

"It's okay? I'm glad it's so easy for you to walk away."

Finally, she shoved her glasses off her face to hold back her windblown hair and let me see the tears shimmering in her eyes. "It's not easy, Max, trust me. I wanted this to work out, but how can it when you don't trust me enough to let me be there for you? Or to not sleep with other men?"

"I said I was sorry."

"You did. If only I could so easily forget being called a biker bunny, or seeing the hatred in your eyes as you said it." Tears fell faster and she didn't bother to get rid of them, she just let them fall down her cheeks and her neck until they finally fell to her shirt or the ground below.

Her tears gutted me, but my frustration at her unwillingness to listen was getting the better of me. "Now I'm not allowed to make a mistake?"

"Of course you are! The problem is that you don't want to correct the mistakes, Max! You plan to spend your life barely sleeping until you lose your mind and hurt yourself, or someone else?" Then she swiped away the tears and took several deep breaths to calm herself.

"I did hurt someone. You! How come you can't see that? I leave to protect you, Jana. Don't you realize that I could have killed you?"

She shook her head, sadness hanging off her like fine jewels. "But you didn't, and honestly, I'm more worried about the damage you're doing to yourself. Max, this isn't easy for me, not at all. I'm in love, for the first time in my life, and the man I love doesn't trust me. Doesn't want me. I'm sorry." More tears fell but it was the soft sniffles that tore me in half.

"No, dammit. This isn't how things were supposed to be. You are supposed to be supportive and stand by me. Or was all that just bullshit so you could seem like the wise old woman who didn't let her scars keep her from living?"

She gasped and took a step back and I immediately regretted my words. When all the fight left her, I knew I'd fucked up bad. "I guess maybe I am, Max. The difference is that I let you and Teddy drag me out once in a while because I knew it came from a place of care and concern. I don't think you can say that, if you're honest with yourself."

I knew I couldn't, but right now my pride wouldn't let me. "So I don't move on your timeline and we're over?"

She let out a sob that kicked me in my heart and my balls at the same time when she dropped the pail and clutched her chest. "Max, I've asked you to stay and instead of just telling me you're worried about your nightmares, you sneak out so you don't have to deal with it. Or you lie about why you can't stay." She shook her head. "It isn't about my timeline, it's about the fact that I don't see it changing and I hate the fact that the first time I took a chance on a man, I wasn't enough." She turned toward the door and I called out to her.

"You are enough, more than enough, Jana. That's why I'm here. I miss you. I'm sorry. I need you."

She sighed and leaned against the doorframe. "I miss you too, Max. More than I miss you when you're here with me lately. Thank you for the memories and for making me feel beautiful. I hope you find what you're looking for." She closed the door so softly I barely heard the click, but I heard the soft thud of her leaning against the door and sliding down.

I sat in that same spot, outside and listened as Jana cried her eyes out. Over me. I should've gotten up and left, gone far the fuck away from the way her tears tore my heart and ripped it to shreds. But I couldn't move; I was held captive by her pain. Eyes closed, I leaned my head on the door as she cried and cried, barely stopping to catch her breath. Eventually the tears stopped and I stood, frozen and confused. I wanted to force my way in and wrap my arms around her to console her, but I also wanted to flee from the feelings Jana stirred in me.

"I'm sorry, Jana."

And I was. A sorry son of a bitch because everything she said was right on the fucking money. With one last look at her door, I left. With a plan that started and ended with proving Jana wrong.

Chapter 16

Jana

"You have to stop sulking." Teddy started in as soon as I answered the phone, and I didn't bother trying to hide the eye roll she couldn't see.

"I'm not sulking. I'm working." That was true, mostly. I did have a lot of work to do because I'd taken on three new clients this week, small businesses that needed my help. And because I was doing my best to ignore the pain in my chest, the constant desire to cry and the face that flashed in my mind at least a million times a day. Work was my jam, where I excelled in life. Work was clean and easy, and everything usually made perfect sense, so I threw myself into it with the intensity of someone who had nothing but her career, working late into the night until I fell in an exhausted heap into bed.

"They aren't mutually exclusive, Jana."

I let out a frustrated groan. "Agreed but since I'm not sulking, it's a moot point." Besides I was doing a lot more than working. "I'm finishing up my sketches for the art show, smartass."

She laughed as she always did when I fought back because Teddy was as strange as she was beautiful. "You're being secretive about it and it's got me curious."

"We both know that's never a good thing," I told her with a laugh, but the truth was, I did have a reason for keeping quiet on the subject. "I want to ask you something. Feel free to say no. I want to sketch your legs."

The other line went silent just as I knew it would. Teddy was strong, she was a badass, but she was also insecure as hell about her legs. It was a sore spot for her and asking might change our friendship.

"It's all right, Teddy. Really. I have a self-portrait as the centerpiece of the collection, titled 'Beauty & Pain.' If you say no, I'll do something else." After hours spent staring at my reflection and thinking about how

I'd probably be alone forever, I was emotionally drained. Usually I hated self-portraits because looking into a mirror was at the very bottom of my list of fun activities, but with everything else that had happened, sketching myself had been cleansing and the end result was...good art. "It's just a sketch, but your legs are fantastic and they would make a great subject."

"I know friends are supposed to make you feel better, but 'fantastic' is a bit of a stretch, don't you think?"

I shook my head even though she couldn't see me. "No, I don't. They're beautiful, period. The scar doesn't take away from that."

She laughed bitterly. "Too bad you can't see that when you look in the mirror. But I'm saying yes because I hope you can see the same beauty in your face that you see in my legs."

I laughed. "Thanks, Teddy. You're the best."

"I know. But don't think I'm standing next to it during the show like some freak show."

This time I laughed outright because my friend was nuts. "Never. Hell, I'm hoping for a wardrobe malfunction that will make me so late that it'll be pointless to show up at all." I wished for it every morning, but Moon had worked hard on this show and I couldn't let her down. I would be there, awkward and uncomfortable, but there. "Are you calling me to put off your own work?"

"Yes. No. Maybe." She let out a heavy sigh. "The groom wants fish as part of the theme, Jana. *Fish!* Dammit, hang on." The phone went silent but not dead, but after a few minutes I hung up and went back to finishing up the sketch I was working on until my muscles began to ache. A long bath loosened me up but it also created unwanted tension as my thoughts wandered to Max and his poor opinion of me. To Max and waking up with his hands around my throat. I didn't blame him for the PTSD but I did blame him for pretending it was all under control when it wasn't.

I knew my life was out of control when being choked by a man hurt less than knowing that man thought I hunted for biker cock and would hop from the bed of one brother to the other. Even if I had the ability to be that woman, I wouldn't and the fact that Max didn't know that, fucking hurt. Then again, he accused me of being someone I'm not, so maybe he was doing the same thing.

I'd always believed that it was better to know what people thought of me up front, but knowing just how low his opinion of me was, considering all that we'd talked about and done together, hurt like hell. It didn't dry my tears faster and it sure as fuck didn't satisfy the aching, burning sensation in my chest.

That meant it was time to pull on my big girl panties and get back to life as usual.

KB Winters

Chapter 17

Max

"I can't believe all the shit I said to her. Hearing it back from her and seeing the devastation all over her face, made me feel like a complete asshole."

I'd been in Dr. Singh's office for more than an hour and we were no closer to any fucking solutions. "Now she won't talk to me or take my calls. And she hasn't been in class for two straight weeks. What if she's not leaving the house, Doc?"

Singh, true to his nature, sat there as calm as could be. His breathing was even and his dark eyes were kind and sympathetic. "We can talk about that, but I'd like to talk about why you said those things to her."

"Shit, Doc, really?" I raked a hand through my hair and then scrubbed it over my face, letting out a long, harsh sigh. "If you ask my brother he'd say I was jealous. Jana probably thinks I'm an asshole. Both of them are no doubt right."

"The fact that you're admitting to having any feelings is progress, Max. When you first came to me all you would say was that you were 'fine.' Everything was 'fine' and you were only here to appease your friend Brandt. This is good."

Shit, listening to Singh I realized just how much I'd buried my head in the sand. "Shit. What you're saying is that it's my fault I'm still having these nightmares." It wasn't a question because I knew the answer. I could see it clearly now. I came here every week, talked about shit, but never tried to fix anything.

"No. I'm saying that *war* is the reason you're still having nightmares. You are the reason they haven't lessened in intensity." He said this in a kind, almost bland way, but that didn't take the sting out of the sentiment. "Are you willing to try another form of therapy or maybe medicine?"

"Not meds," I barked out. "I don't want to be a fucking zombie, Doc. I need to be myself, to be able to function. Anything but drugs."

"Anything?"

The challenge in his question had me on edge but I nodded anyway. "Yeah, anything." With a wide smile, Dr. Singh told me about several alternative treatments, explaining the benefits and drawbacks of each one. There was so much fucking information my head began to swim. "Now you're making me wish I chose the drugs."

He laughed and shook his head. "If you're that against the drugs, we'll stay away from them. There are plenty of other options to explore first." He scribbled out some shit on a pad of paper and handed it to me. "Call this number and set up an appointment."

I gave the paper a skeptical look but nodded. "Sure. Thanks."

"Max, the important thing is that you're dedicated to lessening the effects of your PTSD."

I heard what he said and nodded again. "Got it. Thanks." After shaking his hand, I hopped on my bike and drove away from the low brick building. Home was my destination but I took the route in the opposite direction just to check on Jana. Her car was parked in the same spot it had been for the past week so I drove past and made my way home.

Leaving her alone was probably the best thing I could do for her, but it fucking sucked for me. Jana had crawled under my skin; she'd gotten to me in a way no one ever had. Hell, in a way I didn't think anyone ever could. I knew I had to make this right, but I had no fucking clue how. And worse, I had no clue where to even begin looking for an answer.

Inside the house I found Tate lying on the sofa and staring up at the ceiling. "Find any answers up there? Because I could use a few myself."

His mouth curved up but otherwise he didn't move. "Bad day with the head shrinker?"

"The opposite, actually. The problem is it'll take more than an apology to get Jana fucking talking to me again." I dropped down on the chair and crossed my legs on the old coffee table, wishing I'd stopped by the kitchen for a beer first. "She was right about a lot of the shit she said and I'm working on it, but..." Shit. I didn't even know how to finish that sentence. Pathetic.

"But working on it isn't good enough when you consider all the shit you threw at her?" His lips twitched with amusement.

"Yeah, basically. You don't have to enjoy this so much, you know."

He sat up and shrugged. "I don't have to, but it's a nice change of pace, seeing you out of sorts. Growing up you were always so damn unflappable, cool under pressure. And now a tiny wisp of a thing is twisting you in knots." His smile changed from amused to wistful. "It's not such a bad thing."

"Having it and losing it, though, fucking sucks." And I just couldn't fucking live with the idea of not seeing Jana again, not holding her or kissing her. Never hearing that sexy, husky laugh that always sent a shot of lust straight through me. "Got any advice? Useful advice," I added when he opened his mouth, closed it and smiled.

"Yeah, go big."

"What the hell does that mean? An engagement ring? An expensive trip?" I didn't make an effort with women, especially outside the bedroom. They were guaranteed a good time, at least one incredible orgasm before I got mine and that was it. "Why isn't an apology enough?"

"Because you said terrible shit to her. Do you think I should take the state of Nevada's apology and forego making them pay for stealing six fucking years from me?"

"You know I don't. Those fuckers messed up and they have all the power, I hope you get their fucking pensions!"

"And Jana deserves less?" He must've seen something pathetic in my eyes because his anger deflated. "You need a big ass gesture to prove to Jana that you're not just sorry but willing to go to extremes to make sure you know how bad you fucked up."

That made a twisted kind of sense. "So, make a fool of myself?"

Tate laughed and raked a hand through his hair. "That always helps, but somehow I don't think that's what Jana would want you to do. Find something that matters and show her how you feel about her. If you know, that is."

I frowned. "What's that supposed to mean?"

Tate stood and shrugged, disappearing into the kitchen and returning with two bottles of beer. "It means if you don't love her, you probably shouldn't bother."

Shit. "Why is it always about love?" I liked Jana, a lot. I had other feelings that were *more* than like but they didn't seem big enough to be love. How the fuck should I know what love is? Other than familial love, for my family and my brothers in arms, I had no idea.

"Because, big brother, love makes the world go 'round. Or so they say. Personally though, you love her and you don't want to be without her, so why deny it?"

Why the fuck, indeed. Love was a big word, a really big one. It was important, all-consuming. Life-changing. "I need to think about this shit. Thanks," I told him and took my beer to my room so I could dig deep into the dark recesses of my mind and figure out if I deserved the kind of light Jana brought with her.

Chapter 18

Jana

Standing in front of my closet in nothing but my lingerie and a robe, I bit my lip and looked at my limited options. Tonight was the art show and my nerves were so frazzled, I felt moments away from a panic attack. I left my phone in the living room just to make sure I didn't call Moon and bail at the last minute. I was really, really tempted.

But in the spirit of big girl panties—black lace, tonight—I stood and stared for something appropriate yet modest, and most important of all, inconspicuous. All of my dress clothes were professional, which meant pencil and A-line skirts, and button up shirts and silky blouses. Basically, it was boring as hell. Boring was my jam because it didn't draw too much attention. Black seemed to be the best option so I pulled out a black skirt and a long sleeved black lace shirt with a black cami underneath. Black on black was perfect and with a reluctant sigh, I set it on the bed.

The bell rang and I groaned because it meant I was running out of time. Teddy was here. Tightening the sash on my robe, I practically marched to the front door and yanked it open. "You're early."

She flashed a grin and breezed right on in, ignoring the scowl on my face. "I know. I had a feeling you might be dragging your ass, and I come bearing gifts!" Teddy's laugh was contagious and it worked to alleviate some of my nerves.

Not all, but some. "Gifts, you say? I hope there's a bottle in one of those bag," I told her nodding toward the garment bag and her tiny sparkly clutch.

"No bottle, but something better." Perfectly sculpted auburn brows wiggled and she turned on her red stilettos and headed to my bedroom.

"Where are you going?"

"You think this bag is for my health? Get your butt in here."

I hesitated for just a moment because Teddy couldn't be put off long. She dealt with difficult clients, no, difficult *brides*, for a living and could out last my stubbornness. She was pulling the zipper on the garment bag when I entered the room with a groan. "You got me clothes? I thought we were friends, *Theodora*."

Her blue eyes narrowed to slits. "You're lucky I love you or you'd be dead right now." She kept her face in a scowl but I saw her lips twitch in amusement moments before she burst out laughing. "Anyway, I have a little black dress just for you, honey."

She held up the dress and—not a shocker—it was gorgeous. Short and black with a scoop neck and a low back. "That back is practically indecent!"

She laughed. "Practically, maybe. But it isn't indecent. All of your bits will be covered, I promise."

I wasn't a believer. The dress looked too small to hold my curves and worse, it might draw too much attention to me. "I don't know, Teddy."

"Trust me." Big blue eyes looked into mine, begging me to trust her and I did trust her. More than anyone.

I rolled my eyes and blew out a long, resigned sigh. "Fine. Give me the damn dress."

She handed it over with a triumphant grin, crossed her arms and waited for me to put it on. "You're going to look so hot." Her smile beamed and she clapped excitedly.

"Let's not go crazy," I told her and pulled the tie on my robe. The dress felt like a cloud, soft and silky smooth as it slid over my body. It wasn't tight but it fit perfectly, almost like a glove. The scoop neck made my neck look long and graceful without making my chest look pornographic. It was shorter than I liked, hitting just above the knee. When I turned to see the back, I was amazed at how sexy it looked. Smooth and touchable—if I wanted to be touched—which I didn't.

"Well, what do you think?"

I could hear the smile in her voice even before I met her gaze in the mirror. "It's too sexy but it's perfect for tonight. With a pashmina, though."

"Of course," she said and rolled her eyes. "But only if you get chilly."

"I'm already chilly with half my back exposed. Is my underwear showing?" I heard her laugh and shook my head. "I love it Teddy, thank you. But I'm not sure I can wear it."

"Of course you can. You'll draw every eye in the house."

"Yeah that's my point. It's bad enough that Moon is going to rope me into talking to people, now you want the ones I can ignore to look at me too? No thanks."

"Well," she began and crossed her arms, telling me she wasn't happy with my gratitude. Or lack of. "You can't wear that, it looks like funeral wear. This is Vegas, not New York, Jana." She shrugged. "I guess you can go with your favorite paint-splattered jeans."

"Ugh, I hate you right now."

She laughed and flashed a victorious grin. "I love you too, now figure out what shoes you want to wear while I set up for hair and makeup." She bent and picked up my velvet burgundy stilettos.

"I guess I'm ready." I had no place that would fit us both so we set up in the kitchen.

"Are you worried that Max will be there?"

"He won't be," I insisted, maybe a little too strongly, but I knew he wouldn't because I hadn't told him about it.

"Then why are you so nervous?" She gently combed my hair, separating it as she spritzed and curled.

"Because I don't like being the center of attention, Teddy. Tonight is all about that and I really don't want to deal with it. But I gave my word so all I can do now is try to endure it." People always stared at my face at the doctor's office, the grocery store and restaurants, but the difference was that tonight I'd be the one putting myself out there to be stared and pointed at. Mocked.

"Don't worry honey, I'll be right beside you all night. If anyone steps out of line, I'll make them regret it. And I might even make them regret being born, just for fun." We laughed because it was true. I'd seen Teddy cut a man with nothing more than her razor-sharp tongue. "Speaking of Max," she began.

"We weren't," I rushed and replied.

"Have you spoken to him at all? Close your eyes."

I did as she ordered and tilted my head back, waiting for the feel of the sponge or brush over my face. It was always a surreal experience when Teddy slathered face paint on me, because I never wore it. It was a pointless exercise, but Teddy wanted to help and this was how she did it.

"No. There's nothing more to say. He refuses to get the help he needs that will make things better, so we can't be together. I love Max and I never thought I'd get to know a man well enough to fall in love with him.

I let him take me out to restaurants and bars because it made him feel better, but he won't even try to get a little better for himself. Or me. Message received."

Loud and fucking clear. It had taken a few days but now I mostly felt numb about it, only crying when I curled up in bed by myself.

Teddy was silent for so long I thought she'd dropped the topic while she finished putting her expensive gunk on my face. But I should've known better. "Jana I'm going to say something you might not like."

I felt my body clench but I would hear her out. "I'm listening."

"It's really hard to come back from something like this."

I scoffed and opened my eyes to find hers far too close. "Yeah, I think I know something about that."

She nodded and set the blush brush down. "You do, but it's not the same. When your trauma happened, you were a child still figuring out who you were going to be in this world. That was a different hardship, but Max was a grown man with a purpose in his life, one that was very dear to his heart. He not only lost that purpose, but he lost it horrifically. Along with some of his best friends, men who were like family to him, who saved his life, went to war beside him."

She took a deep breath and the sympathy swimming in her eyes nearly made me bawl like a baby. "I'm not minimizing what you went through, it was fucking terrible, but I'm just trying to make you understand. It's hard to lose your whole identity."

I listened to her words and processed them, trying to see things from her side. From Max's side. It's true that I was a poor kid with nothing but the foster parents the state entrusted with my care. Robert's actions devastated me, Karen's too. But I didn't have a career to lose yet, or friends vanish from my life.

"It is different, you're right. But I'm not asking him to be healed, because I know there is no complete healing from his trauma. All I'm asking is that he takes steps to decrease his suffering, the frequency of his nightmares. He's not. Instead he goes home instead of staying with me."

I closed my eyes as they began to burn with unshed tears threatening to spill over. I took a deep breath to keep those tears where they were. "Wouldn't he at least try, Teddy? If I mattered at all to him?"

For once in our friendship, she was speechless. That in itself was my answer.

"So." I stood and slipped on my shoes. "Are we ready to get this over with?"

Teddy grinned as she stood and reached for my shoulders. "You mean are we ready for your art world debut? The answer is hell to the yeah!"

Her enthusiasm was contagious and I wore a smile all the way to the art gallery beside Moon's art supply shop.

Stepping inside the crowded gallery, my smile dropped.

Chapter 19

Max

"Are you sure she's gonna show?" Tate stood beside me in the doorway of the art gallery, which was right beside the store where we had class on Friday night. "I don't see her."

"She'll be here. Jana wouldn't do that to Moon." At least I hoped she wouldn't. I looked down at my outfit to make sure I looked all right and instantly I felt like a tool. Jana wouldn't give a shit that I'd dressed up, and she seemed to prefer me in jeans and a t-shirt. When she preferred me at all, that was.

"Dude, is that a cock?" Tate pointed at a large blue statue that, yep, looked just like a cock and balls.

A loud laugh escaped me, drawing the attention of several others inside the gallery. "Looks like it is, though I'd worry if the cock is blue too."

Tate snickered again. "If it's that blue, you're beyond help."

With a shake of my head, I pushed him forward to the next display as my head swiveled back and forth, hoping to catch a glimpse of that white blond hair I knew so well. She hadn't arrived yet, or she was hiding someplace. It gave me time to look around at the gallery. It was sparse with mostly white walls and red brick separating the exhibits. The large room was dimly lit and there didn't seem to be any real order to the place.

"Max." Tate smacked my chest with the back of his hand to get my attention and pointed at the exhibit we stood in front of, wearing a knowing grin.

I turned, and my gaze slammed into a familiar, deep brown gaze, only it wasn't brown. It was damn near black from Jana's sketching pencils. It was a self-portrait, which I knew she hated, and staring at the sketch I could see why. She was still the most beautiful thing in the world to me, but it was all undercut by the sadness swimming in her depths. But the sadness wasn't all I saw; there was her strength, the tension in her clenched jaw served as a reminder that she hated the face that I loved. And in that moment, I knew that Tate was right: I did love Jana. It was all so clear, staring at her face and the detail from the little freckle on the bridge of her nose to the dolphin earring on the upper part of her right ear.

"Damn." It was all so beautiful yet painful.

"She's got talent," Tate said, staring at a set of long legs with a long zipper scar up the outside of one leg that I was sure belonged to Teddy.

Just as I was sure the nondescript torso with the ugly starburst scar right over the heart was supposed to be me. The tattoos and gunshot wounds were missing, but the swirl of hair down the stomach was all me, as was the mole beside the left nipple. "It's amazing."

"It's more than that, man. This shit is gold. Pain and beauty and scars. That shit is life." He squinted at the mangled old hands that gripped a golf club that completed the series.

I had to agree but now, more than ever, I wished I could find Jana. Her series, this glimpse into her soul, told me that I still had a chance. Another quick scan produced Moon and I waved her over. "I'd like to buy the big one."

Her eyes went wide, holding a million questions she had the good manners not to ask as she added a red dot beside the picture. "I knew you were a good man, Max. Whatever the problem is, I'm sure you'll work it out." She glanced around my shoulder at Tate and a wide smile bloomed on her face. "I'm so happy you're free, young man." In an unexpected move, she pulled him into a hug and held him for a long moment. "If you need help getting on your feet, your brother knows where to find me." As quickly as she'd rushed over, Moon hurried off.

Tate grinned. "I like her. The crazy ones always love me."

I smiled and shook my head, unwilling to move on in case Jana stopped to check out her display.

"Who in the hell is that hot ginger?"

I knew who he was talking about before I spotted them, but once I saw Jana and her friend, I smiled as relief drained the tension from my body. "That's Teddy, Jana's best friend."

Tate clapped his hands loudly and, swear to god, licked his chops. "You know I have a weakness for hot girls with boys' names. Wish me luck."

My hand struck out and gripped his shoulder. "Me first." I stepped in front of Tate, but I felt his presence behind me as I made my way to Jana, heart racing and thudding into my throat. "Jana. You look beautiful." I couldn't tear my gaze away from the sexy black dress she wore, hugging her hourglass figure deliciously.

She smiled at the sight of me, but her eyes were still sad. "Max. What are...how did you know about the show?" She glanced at Teddy who held her arms up defensively.

"Don't look at me, I don't even know how to get in touch with him."

"Moon told me a couple weeks ago. In class." Being so close to her for the first time in too damn long, shook me to my core. Her perfume was slightly different tonight, more musky than flowery but just as tempting. She had on makeup that made her brown eyes look bottomless. "Can we talk for a minute?"

Jana looked wary, nibbling her bottom lip before she nodded and fell into step beside me. "Sure." We walked away from the crowd towards the back of the building before she spoke again. "How have you been, Max?"

"Not all that great, Jana. I was an asshole to my girl and now she won't talk to me." A smile ghosted around her lush mouth and that was good enough for me. For now, anyway. "I really am sorry about the shit I said. You were right, I was stuck and unwilling to do shit about it, and I blame my shitty behavior on my lack of sleep. And jealousy."

She blinked. "I would never."

"I know," I cut her off. "You're not that kind of woman and it was my own stupid mind fucking with me." I grabbed her hand and laid it over my heart because I needed her to know how I felt. "It was a lack of sleep combined with my growing feelings for you, and my inability to express those feelings. But none of that was on you and I shouldn't have taken it out on you."

"Thank you for saying that, Max. It means a lot." Tears shimmered in her eyes, but Jana was stronger than she knew, and she willed them back.

"You were right about a lot, actually. I talked to Dr. Singh and he recommended some different treatments we're trying out."

This time her smile was full watt and genuine. "That's wonderful, Max. I am so happy for you." I could tell she meant it and it only made me love her more.

"You made me want to get better, Jana. I want to be better for you, so I can kiss you awake every morning. Reach for you in the middle of the night because I can't wait another minute to have you. That's what I want. Tell me it's not too late."

She opened her mouth to speak but I pressed a finger to them.

"First, let me show you something." I pulled her along until we were damn near at the fire exit before I stopped in front of her, clasping her hand in mine. "I asked Moon if I could do something for tonight." I stepped aside to reveal the painting I'd spent the past few nights working on. "The Doc told me to paint something meaningful, something that brought me peace. This is what came out."

She turned and stared at it, released a little gasp. "Oh Max, it's beautiful!" She didn't turn to look at me because she was captivated by the painting, leaning in to take in all the details. "This is fantastic, the purples and blues…it looks almost velvet."

The awe in her voice had a warmth spreading through me and I found myself smiling. "Thanks. When I close my eyes, this is the thought that brings me peace."

She straightened, mouth slightly open as her big brown eyes stared up at me in awe. "Max, it's so beautiful. And that night...it was magical." Her voice choked up and her eyes grew damp with emotion.

"It was the best damn night of my life, Jana. You were everything I never knew I needed."

One tear fell and her face lit up in a breathtaking smile. "Me too. When you reached out and held my hand, it was the first time a man had just held my hand."

"Jana," I grabbed her hands and pressed them against my heart again, let her feel how it raced. For her. "You know, I came here tonight with one goal. Getting you to forgive me. That was as far as I'd gotten, well that and the painting but only once it was done did I realize what it meant."

Hope shone in her eyes. "Oh yeah?" I was happy to see a little bit of spark and sass back in her eyes.

"Hell yeah. Looking at the sketch of you, seeing the strength you don't even realize you possess. The light that shines inside of you, even after the shit hand you were dealt as a kid, and the way you've made a life for yourself. It's all there in the picture. Or maybe I just see it because I'm in love with you." It wasn't the most elegant way to tell her, but I wasn't an elegant guy.

"I'm sorry, you what?" Eyes wide, she stared up at me completely in shock.

She really didn't know. "I love you. Or more accurately, I'm in love with you. Is that news to you?"

Her head bobbed up and down. "It is. Are you sure?"

I couldn't help but laugh at my adorable little accountant. "I am. I was miserable without you, missing you ate me up inside and it wasn't just the sex or your gorgeous figure. It was your laugh, the way your whole face lights up when you smile." I reached out to her, letting my thumb slide down the silky skin of her cheek. "I love you, Jana. It's that simple for me. I'm getting help and I want you to give me a second chance."

She looked up at me, grinning awkwardly but not trying to hide her face from me.

"I."

She opened her mouth and snapped it shut with a nervous grin.

"I love you too, Max. But I'm scared."

I placed my hands over hers, hoping her touch would calm my racing heart. "You think I'm not? I've never been in love before. This shit is all new to me. But I want to be with you. I want to see if we can work, the right way this time."

"What is the right way?" Her question was genuine, and I had to smile because I had no real clue.

"I don't know, but I think we can make our own rules. I'll stay two nights a week to start and more as the nightmares lessen. Or fade."

"Max." The way she sighed my name, like I was something precious to her had me drawing closer, placing my hands on her hips. "You mean it?"

"I do. You think I don't want to wake up with you in my arms every morning? Because I do, so damn bad."

"I'd like that."

Fuck yeah! Her soft, affectionate smile hit me right where it counted. "Yeah?"

"Hell yeah." She bridged the final step between us and wrapped her arms around my waist, pressing her face into my chest. I heard the sniffles she tried to hide and smiled to myself as she looked up at me. "I thought I'd never see you again, or hold you like this Max. I'm glad you came back."

"I couldn't have possibly done anything else, Jana. You're it for me. In fact," I leaned forward and whispered in her ear. "You're kind of stuck with me."

"Since I love you back, I guess you're stuck with me too."

I wrapped my arms around her and pressed her against the wall right beside the painting that had put me on the path to healing. "Sweetheart, there's no place

I'd rather be." And then I touched my lips to hers and kissed her like she was everything, my woman, my lover, my heart, my light. And my love. She was all those things and so much more and I would make sure she knew that.

Every. Damn. Day.

Chapter 20

Jana

"You really are disgusting, you know that don't you?" Teddy dropped down onto a lounge in the backyard, her long shapely legs on display in a knee-length summer dress. The yellow and white polka dots were at odds with her sophisticated up do, but matched perfectly with her sun kissed skin and freckled shoulders. "I mean, I'm happy for you and all, but seriously." She rolled her eyes and slid the sunglasses over her blue eyes, but I saw the twitch of her lips.

"I think it'll be a nice surprise." Six months had passed since Max and I declared our love for each other and things were damn near perfect. I couldn't have asked for a better man than Max Ellison. He always made me feel beautiful and desirable. Wanted.

"How is that," she pointed at the wooden slats surrounding the newly planted vegetable garden, "a nice surprise?"

"You'll see," I told her as I manned the grill. Max and Tate were coming home today. They'd been in Reno for a few days so Tate and his lawyers could argue that he should be compensated for his wrongful conviction. It was a travesty they didn't automatically pay exonerees, but I had hopes that Tate would win. "I made a pitcher of lemonade if you're thirsty."

Teddy groaned as she got up and poured a glass. "Lemonade," she scoffed. "I don't know if I like this new you," she grinned into her glass and promptly groaned as the boozy cocktail hit her taste buds. "Damn, I still love you girl."

I laughed and rolled my eyes, moving the steaks around the grill and turning over the fish. "I thought you might."

"You thought she might what?"

I turned at the sound of Max's voice with an excited grin for him and Tate. "Hey guys! How'd it go?" I stopped in front of Tate and waited.

"Fantastic. They're working up a settlement agreement as we speak."

"That's great!" I wrapped my arms around his big body and squeezed tight. "I'm so happy for you, Tate."

"Yeah, thanks babe. What smells good?" He sniffed the air and moved toward the grill while I drew closer to Max.

Big, delicious, manly Max. "Teddy will show you where everything is, won't you?"

With an exaggerated eye roll, she stood and waved for Tate to follow her. "You have three minutes," she whispered as she breezed on by.

Max frowned. "Three minutes? That's just enough time to get you all wet and juicy." I felt my skin blush at his words and I cringed. Six months later and the man could still make me feel like a virginal schoolgirl.

"I have a surprise for you, but if you want to go with your thing, I'm game." Cupping his face gently, I pressed a hard kiss to his mouth. "I missed you."

"Not as much as I missed you."

I loved to hear him say things like that, but I really loved it when he got that intense expression on his face that told me just how much he meant that. "I have a surprise for you."

"A surprise like those magic brownies to help me sleep or like that blue lingerie?"

Another blush stained my cheeks and I buried my face in his chest at the memory of that lingerie. I'd never been so bold in my life, but he'd stayed overnight for five straight days and on the sixth I'd worn the most outrageous lingerie I've ever owned. It was a fun night. "Neither, actually." I grabbed his hand and pulled him to the small garden area. "It's a salsa garden."

He frowned in confusion and dropped my hand, but I didn't panic. I knew, with absolute certainty, that Max would love this. Especially when he finally saw the sign that read, 'Garcia's Bomb Ass Salsa Garden'. "You did this for me?"

I nodded. "The experts say that remembering the good things is the key to overcoming a trauma and though it's never worked for me, I think it could work for you. This way every time we eat salsa, it'll be Garcia's."

He stood and wrapped me in his arms. "Is that why you planted the brown eyed Susan's? Because I told you about Reilly's favorite spot on the family ranch?"

"Yep."

"I love the hell out of you Jana. You are the best damn thing that ever happened to me."

"And you are more than I imagined I could ever have out of this life, Max."

He kissed me long and tender, sweet. When he pulled back he wore a nervous smile. "I was going to wait and make it really special, but this seems like the perfect time."

"For what?"

He reached into his pants pocket and pulled out a small velvet box and my breath caught. He flashed a knowing smile that made my heart race. "This. Jana Carson, hottest, sweetest, most amazing woman on the planet, will you do me the great honor of becoming my wife?"

In a million years, I hadn't expected Max to take this step, to *want* to take this step. Marriage, for me, had always been a pipe dream so now, in this important moment in my life, I could only stare at the gorgeous emerald cut diamond that did its best to outshine the Nevada sun.

"Don't leave me hanging sweetheart."

I blinked and looked up at those amazing gray eyes with a shaky smile. "Oh Max, I can't wait to be your wife. Yes, I'll marry you!" I jumped in his arms as tears slipped down my cheeks, feeling happier than I could ever remember feeling in my whole life. This man, so strong and sensitive, was all mine.

Forever.

"Oh boy, they're at it again," Teddy said, breaking the spell we'd woven around ourselves.

"We were celebrating," I told her, pulling Max beside me as we stopped in front of Teddy and Tate. "We are officially engaged."

Teddy squealed as I knew she would, wrapping both of us in her lean arms. "Congratulations guys!"

I basked in her praise and her affection along with Tate's and the feel of Max's steady hand at my back, had me full to bursting with love.

It took a long time—a lot of therapy and acceptance—to get here but these three people were now my family.

In every sense of the word.

* * * *

~ THE END ~

Acknowledgements

Thank you! I love you all and thank you for making my books a success!! I appreciate each and every one of you.

Thanks to all of my beta readers, street teamers, ARC readers and Facebook fans. Y'all are THE BEST!

And a huge very special thanks to my wonderful assistants and PA. Without you, I'd be a *hot mess! I'm still a hot mess, but without your keen sense of organization and skills, I'd be a burny fiery inferno of hot mess!! Thank you!

And a very special thanks to my editors (who sometimes have to work all through the night! *See HOT MESS above!) Thank you for making my words make sense.

Copyright © 2018 BookBoyfriends Publishing LLC

KB Winters

About The Author

KB Winters has an addiction to caffeine, tattoos and hard-bodied alpha males. The men in her books are very sexy, protective and sometimes bossy, her ladies are…well…*bossier*!

Living in sunny Southern California, the embarrassingly hopeless romantic writes every chance she gets!

Printed in Great Britain
by Amazon